Meet the Kids at West Mount High . . .

Blake Farraby: Son of a doctor. "Grades are *everything* around my house." Dates Susan Brantley, sometimes. Has a bad case of unrequited love for a red Corvette.

Susan Brantley: Every guy's dream date. Dying to fall in love. "You car is, like, your identity." Could go for a guy in a red Corvette. Recipient of mysterious love letters.

Jesse McCracken: Strong, silent type. Drives the junkiest heap in school. "All day and all night my blood sings Susan. Susan . . ." Not above sabotage to steal a kiss from the girl he loves.

Michael Dessaseaux: World-class couch potato. Loves old movies and his motorcycle. "Greta Garbo . . . wow!" Falls hard for an older woman.

Ann Lee Smith: Quiet, serious, shy. Susan's best friend. "I care about things like thermonuclear war."

Rainey Locklear: Exotic, a freethinker. Calls a trailer park home. "I'm one-half Lumbee Indian." Knows what she wants . . . and goes after it.

Wild Times At WEST MOUNT HIGH

Janice Harrell

AN ARCHWAY PAPERBACK
Published by POCKET BOOKS

New York   London   Toronto   Sydney   Tokyo   Singapore

This book is a work of fiction. Names, characters, places and incidents are either the product of the author's imagination or are used fictitiously. Any resemblance to actual events or locales or persons, living or dead, is entirely coincidental.

AN ARCHWAY PAPERBACK *Original*

An Archway Paperback published by
POCKET BOOKS, a division of Simon & Schuster Inc.
1230 Avenue of the Americas, New York, NY 10020

ISBN: 0-671-68570-8

First Archway Paperback printing December 1989

10   9   8   7   6   5   4   3   2

AN ARCHWAY PAPERBACK and colophon
are registered trademarks of Simon & Schuster Inc.

Printed in the U.S.A.

IL 6+

Wild Times At
WEST MOUNT HIGH

ONE

A Corvette the color of a fine ripe tomato made its way sedately down Sunset Avenue.

"Look how responsive she is," said the salesman. He squirmed eagerly in the passenger seat. "Nothing spongy about this steering, Dr. Farraby."

The older man shook his head. "I don't know."

"It's a lot of car for the money, sir."

"It's a lot of money, that's for sure."

The salesman winced. It looked as if it had been a mistake to bring up money.

Dr. Farraby steered the Corvette into the dealer's lot, parked it, and handed the keys back to the salesman.

"I could hold it for you if you'd like your son to come look at it," the salesman said quickly.

"No, no. Don't do that. The more I think about the car, the more I think it's a bad idea. When you hand kids everything on a silver platter, they start believing the world owes them a living. I worked for everything I ever got, and it did me good.''

The salesman listened respectfully as the doctor expounded on the theme of hard work and deprivation and how they built character.

"Don't hold the car," Dr. Farraby said, concluding his lecture. "I'm rethinking this."

As Dr. Farraby walked away, the salesman let fly a parting shot. "Remember, sir, they're only young once!"

Dr. Farraby didn't turn around. The salesman watched as the doctor drove his Mercedes out of the lot. It had looked like an easy sale—a boy's sixteenth birthday coming up, his father having plenty of money. It was hard for him to believe he had blown it.

On the other side of town a school bus bumped down a red clay road. It had already covered several miles picking up kids, and the noise inside was like that of a jet at takeoff. When the bus stopped at the Starlight Trailer Park, Rainey Locklear climbed aboard, cringing a little as the two door flaps snapped shut behind her. She noticed at once that the Tyler twins were still wearing their lucky socks. They had been wearing them during the West Mount Tigers' victorious game against the East Gate Hornets and vowed not to wash them as long as the team won. Catching the distinctly ripe smell that rose from the twins' feet, Rainey fervently hoped the Tigers would lose their next game.

She sat in one of the few remaining seats. The bus took off with a jolt, and droplets of cola rained down on her white blouse.

"Jeez, Rainey," said Marty Hobson, disgusted. "Half my Coke is all over you."

"Sorry," she murmured automatically. Marty had obviously never heard of a well-balanced breakfast. She didn't know how he could face peanuts and Coke at just past seven in the morning. Even the smell made her queasy.

The bus stopped at Meadowbrook Estates and a large group of kids got on. The last two girls were not familiar to Rainey, sophomores, probably, and both built like hockey goalies. As they passed, one of them dumped her books on Rainey's head. "Oops!" she said. Rainey's head rang from the blow.

The girls giggled as they moved down the aisle. Rainey gritted her teeth and pressed herself back against the seat cushion, wishing she could disappear into it.

The bus lurched ahead. Inside, the air was warm and close from the breath of seventy kids. They were sitting three to a seat now. Some were standing. Rainey noticed with distaste that the guy next to her was not particular about his personal hygiene. Worse, someone near her had practically bathed in Brut. It was very possible that she was getting a sick headache.

As the bus turned onto the highway and proceeded sluggishly toward the high school, Rainey closed her eyes and tried to blot out the noise. The monotonous vibrations of the engine shuddered through her.

Finally the bus pulled into the parking lot at West Mount High. Kids pushed impatiently to the front. A paper airplane sailed past Rainey's nose.

"Move it," the boy next to her said. "We don't have all day."

"In a minute. Hang on."

Rainey bent over and pretended to tie the laces of her sneakers. When she spotted the hockey goalie types approaching, she stuck her foot into the aisle. The largest girl tripped on it and her books went flying.

"I'm so sorry!" Rainey cried. "Here, let me help you up. Goodness, what a shame. You skinned your knee and everything!"

The huge girl glowered menacingly as she retrieved her books, but Rainey was pretty sure she would not drop any books on her next time.

"Come on," said the boy beside Rainey. "Are you going to camp here, or what?"

She got up and joined the slow-moving line of kids. She wondered how she could possibly endure another year of riding the bus.

When she stepped outside, she squinted in the bright light, her long blue-black hair shooting points of fire in the sunshine. She was slight, a mere five-one, but when she squared her shoulders she could look impressive. "I've got to get a car," she murmured. She didn't have the money for a car, but she wouldn't let that discourage her. Rainey had never been a slave to circumstances. She believed in making her own luck.

In the section of West Mount called Applewood, where stately houses sat cloistered on manicured emerald lawns, Susan Brantley stood in her family's three-car garage, looking critically at the paneled station wagon parked next to her mother's shiny new Buick.

"Have you got everything now, Susan? Lunch money?" Her mother, dressed in a bright floral bathrobe, was at the door to the kitchen.

"How do you expect me to think about lunch money? Look at my car!" Susan said, taking a few steps toward her mom. "It's pitiful. Do you know that when Mr. Sanford showed a slide of a station wagon to my psychology class, it was voted the *least* sexy car in the entire sample? The bottom of the barrel! How do you think that makes me feel? Can you see what it's going to do to me to drive it? Guys are going to look at it and say, like, forget it. Mom, this is a matronly car. This is the kind of car you take your kids to kindergarten in.''

''Well, I am a matron and I did take my kids to kindergarten in it,'' said her mother. ''You seemed pretty happy to get it when I bought the new car this summer.''

''But that was before I saw all the implications. Don't you see what the survey in my psych class means? It means that the kind of car you have affects the way guys think about you. Your car is, like, your identity.'' She glanced back at the old station wagon. ''Can't we trade up?''

''No,'' her mother said. ''We cannot. And if you're sure you have your lunch money, I'd like to put a load in the washer.''

Great, thought Susan as she slid her keys into the ignition. *I'm going to be a social outcast. The senior boys will never look at me. And does my mother care? She most emphatically does not!*

Jesse McCracken lived right across the street from the Starlight Trailer Park, but unlike Rainey he didn't have to get up early to wait for the bus. Some time after the bus had gone, he strolled outside to get into his car. ''Aw, move, Blue. Get out of here. Mom, would you call Blue?''

''Just say good morning to her, Jesse. That's all she wants. Come here, Blue.''

The McCrackens had six yard dogs, all of them good

hunting dogs, except for Blue. Since puppyhood, Blue had been uninterested in chasing deer, squirrels, turkeys, rabbits, or anything else edible. Furthermore, he was ugly, with large liver-colored spots all over him. Most of his time was spent following the McCrackens around and licking their faces. He had a habit of standing in front of them and gazing up with adoring brown eyes. They were always tripping over him. Jesse's father said he was embarrassed to be feeding such a worthless hound, but the truth was they all loved Blue. It was one of life's ironies that it was Blue who was the cause of Jesse's unhappiness.

Jesse knew that the way he looked didn't give a clue as to how bitter he found life that sunny Monday morning. The khaki pants his mother had bought him still had the original creases in them, his sneakers were unsmudged, his sun-bleached hair was swept cleanly back from his forehead, and his gray eyes were clear and steady. *For neatness give me a ten,* he thought bitterly. *For peace of mind, give me a zero.*

He got in the passenger side of the car and slid across to the wheel because the door on the driver's side didn't open. He drove in a semicircle through the rutted front yard. The chickens fluttered around like imbeciles as he drove past their coop. He pulled out onto the red clay road in front of the house and sped away, leaving a thick cloud of dust behind him.

Jesse's expression seldom hinted at what was going on in his mind. He had spent the entire summer driving a tractor on his uncle's farm, without anyone knowing that he was nursing a hopeless love. He had loaded bales of hay until his back ached, sweated in the heat, drunk buckets of iced tea, and slapped endless mosquitoes. Every

Sunday he had gone to church and then back to his grand-parents' house for a family gathering with great quantities of fried chicken, biscuits, mashed potatoes, gravy, and field peas. As long as he went through the motions of maintaining a normal schedule, no one suspected anything was wrong. His family would have been astonished to know that all he thought about all the time was Susan. He dreamed of her and brooded over his hopeless love constantly, like a duck over a nest of eggs.

He pulled his old car out into the highway, frowning fiercely. Why did people going fifty have to block the fast lane? "Out of my way, idiot, " he muttered. He hit his horn with his fist. When the slow-moving Volks-wagen took the hint and moved to the right lane, Jesse stepped on the gas and sped past it. A few miles later he exited at twice the posted speed. "I've got to snap out of this," he muttered.

When he arrived at the large painted sign that said "West Mount High School," he was forced to join the line of cars inching toward the school parking lot. It was painful to have to go so slow. And it struck him that his mind was like his car engine, racing and unable to move. No matter what he thought about, he kept coming back to Susan. He could almost see her—the gold hoops in her ears flashing in the light, her blond hair, crinkled like an angel's on a Victorian Christmas card, the faint blue veins at her wrist. . . .

From every direction cars with green West Mount High parking stickers were approaching the lot, their tape decks blaring competing music. A guy in a Ford GT rolled down his window and yelled at somebody. A distant horn sounded. It was a completely normal morning. Jesse wished he could do something to release the pressure inside him—scream, maybe, or fling open the car door and run out into the woods. But he knew he wouldn't. Jesse, the iceman, he thought bitterly.

His unhappiness had begun one sultry Saturday afternoon the previous spring, when his father had pulled into the Burger King parking lot. Blue, as usual, was riding in the back of the pickup, looking out over the side of the truck bed with his tongue hanging out. The dog in the next car barked and Blue answered him with spirit. Suddenly there was a menacing growl and Ben McCracken looked up to a flash of white filling his rearview mirror for a second. He turned and through the back window saw a big white dog on top of Blue, ripping his belly. Blue's screams were horrible. Ben McCracken grabbed his rifle, jumped out of the truck cab, and fired twice. The white dog jerked twice and dropped.

Ben climbed up on the truck bed and pulled the white dog off Blue. He laid his hand on the hound's head to comfort him. He could see that Blue was in shock. "Hang on, ole boy," he said, tears springing to his eyes. "We're going to get you to the vet."

Susan's dad came running out of the Burger King. Ben McCracken lifted the limp corpse of the white dog and dropped it off the truck bed at Mr. Brantley's feet. "I'm sorry, mister, but you had a vicious dog there."

"Murderer!" screamed Mr. Brantley. "You'll pay for this, you trigger-happy redneck." He broke off with a sob. "You killed him. You killed poor Muffin. I'll get you for this. Don't think you're going to get away with it. People like you ought to be locked up, and I'm going to see to it that you are, don't you worry."

"Excuse me," said Ben McCracken. "I've got to get my dog to the vet." He pushed past Brantley, got in his truck, and slammed the door closed. Brantley banged on the side of the truck with his fist as Ben McCracken pulled out of the parking space. Driving away, McCracken could see Brantley in the rearview mirror. He was standing over the white dog, his hands balled into fists.

A few days later the McCrackens went to the vet's to visit Blue. He was sedated to keep him from ripping out his stitches, and it broke Jesse's heart to see him lying there, drooling and out of it. Jesse almost didn't know what was worse, seeing Blue in such bad shape or realizing that what had happened ended everything between Susan and him.

At the end of the week Blue came home from the veterinary hospital. Ben McCracken paid a thirty-five-dollar fine for discharging a firearm within city limits, and Jesse and his family assumed the incident was officially over.

But it wasn't. Susan's dad was a member of the city council. He had a means of revenge. A building permit was issued quietly, and one morning in June, the Mc-Crackens woke to see a bulldozer pushing down the half acre of pine trees across from their house. They watched in dismay as the stripped earth was paved and plumbing and wiring outlets installed. Finally a sign with flashing purple and pink lights appeared—"Starlight Trailer Park."

The McCrackens tried to pretend the cement lot wasn't there, but before long it was packed with trailers. A truck rumbled down the road at four every morning to empty the park's fly-infested Demster Dumpster. When it lifted the dumpster, it made unearthly creaking and groaning noises that always woke the McCrackens. Worse, the people at the trailer park had an assortment of ill-trained little dogs who stood on their cement patch all day barking challenges at the McCrackens' hunting dogs.

After a while Jesse's mother started noticing police cars at the trailer park. It seemed to her that the police were over there fairly often. She supposed they were searching for stolen property or intervening in noisy domestic disputes. Normally, she called on new neighbors and welcomed them with a plate of brownies, but she couldn't bring herself to call on any of the people at the trailer park.

"We could move," she suggested. But Jesse knew it would never happen. They lived on the remnant of a farm that had been in the McCracken family for a hundred years, and there was no way Ben McCracken would sell. Whenever Jesse's mom brought up the subject, his dad drew his lips into a thin line and went outside to clean his guns, his favorite occupation when he needed to calm himself.

Jesse was forced to accept that he was in the middle of what amounted to a blood feud. The whole situation was so tense that he couldn't even speak to Susan anymore, much less ask her out.

Whenever he thought about it, he choked with anger. He only wished he knew who to punch out. Why did this have to happen to him? Looking around him, he took a deep breath and inhaled the carbon monoxide the other cars in the line were spewing out. For the hundredth time he wondered what he had ever done to deserve such bad luck.

At least the traffic was starting to move. One of the teachers directing traffic spoke into his walkie-talkie and motioned for the right lane to begin turning into the parking lot.

Not far behind Jesse's car was the white Volvo driven by Blake Farraby's mother.

"At last we're starting to move," said Mrs. Farraby. "I don't understand why there have to be so many cars. When I was in high school the parking lot was nothing— it was tiny. Hardly anybody had cars."

"Well, everybody has a car now," Blake said pointedly. *Everybody but me,* he thought. He slumped down in the seat, hoping nobody would notice that he was being driven to school by his mother.

His sixteenth birthday was less than two weeks away. At his most optimistic, he had dreamed that his parents would give him a car as a birthday present, but lately he had the feeling it wasn't going to happen. He was sensitive to his father's moods and just knew he was fated to spend his junior and senior years as a pedestrian.

Blake's parents had no understanding of the bind they had put him in. He would have happily bought a car himself if he could have, but they wouldn't let him have an after-school job because they wanted to be sure he kept his grades up. Good grades were a mania with them.

He remembered the time in the seventh grade when he let his homework slip because he had been spending a lot of time at basketball practice. Just playing on the team had been a big thrill for him. Not that it was any great honor—you didn't even have to try out for basketball in the seventh grade. He just liked being out there with the other guys. He worshiped Coach Briggs. When the coach said, "Eat good red meat," Blake ate good red meat. When the coach said to save your swearing for the locker room, Blake tried. Every afternoon he went out in the driveway and shot baskets. He wasn't a natural, but he had his moments. Once, he had scored three times in one game. He would never forget it—that crazy giddy feeling that he might be the next Larry Bird.

But when report cards came out at the end of the six weeks, an ominous silence fell over the Farraby household. Blake's parents retreated to their bedroom to confer. That night they sat him down after dinner for a blunt talk.

"I am five foot ten," Dr. Farraby had said. "Your mother is five foot three. Think about that, son. Consider the laws of heredity. You are never going to be a famous basketball player."

Blake had squirmed. "It's just for fun, Dad."

Mrs. Farraby had smoothed some pieces of computer paper out on the dining table. "Look at these, Blake. These are your CAT scores. If you couldn't do the work, your father and I wouldn't say a word—would we, Richard? But you can do it, and we can't stand here and watch you ruin your life."

"It's up to you, son. Are you going to be serious about school or are you just going to fritter away your time?"

"We're only saying this because we love you, Blake. You've got to start thinking about your future. Look at your grade in math! Only the top ten percent are going to make it into eighth-grade algebra and if you aren't in that ten percent you'll have to wait for the ninth grade to take algebra. If that happens, you won't have time to take all the math courses you'll need to get into engineering or premed in college!"

"It's not that we're telling you what to do with your life. We only want you to keep your options open."

"We don't want you to waste your talents."

Blake quit the basketball team the next day. Even now, thinking about it depressed him.

"You can let me off here, Mom," Blake said.

"I can get you up a lot closer that this. Hold on. I'll drop you right up there where all those kids are."

"No!" he yelped. "I told you. Let me off right here!"

"Please, Blake, wait till I stop before you get out. Do you want to get killed?"

Blake slammed the car door behind him. He stooped to pick up the book he had dropped in his wild lunge from the car and looked around him like a hunted man. It was bad enough to be dropped off at school by your mommy, but to have *everyone* in school see you—that was worse.

He sauntered through the parking lot toward the portico where the mob of kids was standing. He was trying his best to look as if he had just stepped out of his own personal Jag, but he was afraid he wasn't succeeding.

"Hey, watch where you're going, Farraby."

Blake had banged his books up against Jesse Mc-Cracken's old heap. Jesse dusted the grill protectively with his hand.

"Sorry," Blake muttered. Jesse's car was the most disreputable one in the parking lot. It looked as if it had been painted with peanut butter. And though Jesse had worked hard hammering dents out of it, he had only succeeded in making the chassis look shapeless. *If Methuselah had had a car, this might have been it,* thought Blake.

Blake stared at the car without blinking, and all of a sudden he had a blinding flash. A revelation! He was almost afraid to move lest the bloom come off his wonderful idea.

"Jesse," he choked out, "would you be interested in selling your car?"

Jesse took a step back and regarded him with narrowed eyes. "Maybe," he said cautiously. "For the right price."

"My grandfather sent me some savings bonds for my birthday," said Blake quickly. "I think we can work something out."

"It's been well maintained. I've babied this sucker."

"Oh, I know. I know."

Jesse's gray eyes surveyed the sky over the school building. "I wouldn't take a penny less than five hundred for it," he said loftily.

"Two hundred."

"Three-fifty."

"Deal."

Jesse figured the car was actually worth something in the neighborhood of two hundred, if you counted the sentimental value as well as the value of the tires and the jack in the trunk. He began to feel funny about the deal and looked at Blake uneasily. Blake was smoothing his dark hair with both hands, and his expression was one that Jesse couldn't quite fathom. He looked—excited.

"Now, look, you aren't just going to trash it or anything, are you?" Jesse asked suddenly. "Because I'm kind of attached to it."

"Trash it? No way. I'm going to drive it."

"Well, they don't make them like this anymore." On one hand, Jesse felt as if he were taking advantage of Blake, and on the other he sort of hated to part with his car, even though it was falling apart.

Blake ran his finger around the inside of his collar. "I'll take good care of it, Jesse. Honest. Can you bring me the title tomorrow?"

"You bring the money, and I'll bring the title."

14

The bell went off like a bomb, making even the usually nerveless Jesse jump. The two boys strode off toward the mob surging in through the east entrance.

"Blake!" A girl with crimped blond hair struggled toward them. When Jesse saw her he went rigid. It was Susan.

She grabbed Blake's arm. "Look, in trig were we supposed to do the odd-numbered problems or the even-numbered? I did the odd-numbered, but last night I had bad dreams about it. Now I'm not so sure I wrote down the right ones."

Jesse watched Susan's heaving bosom with painful fascination. He could have gazed at her all day except that when he did he felt a little lightheaded and was afraid he might pass out.

"Calm down," Blake said. "It was the odd ones."

Susan sighed in relief.

"I think," added Blake mischievously.

A motorcycle roared into the lot behind them.

"There's Michael," said Susan. "Running late as usual."

She and Blake waited while a big guy with tousled hair parked his bike and limped over to them. "Took a spill in my driveway," he panted.

"I hope you don't kill yourself on that thing," said Susan.

She was nice to everyone, thought Jesse, moving on, even crazy Michael Dessaseaux. But not to him. Her eyes rested briefly on him, but they looked right through him. Stoically, he inched his way into the school building. He felt as if his heart had risen to his throat and was stuck there. Of course, he thought sourly, Blake was the kind she would go for. Susan and Blake lived in the same neighborhood. They probably went to debutante teas, or whatever you called them, and shared sips of martinis on their families' patios. Thinking about that, he almost began to dislike Blake. Normally, he wouldn't have felt outclassed by Blake, but these were not normal times. Nothing had been normal since that afternoon Susan's dog had jumped Blue.

When Jesse reached his locker, his old girlfriend, Terri, was standing in front of it with a funny, set expression on her face. Jesse had to control the cowardly impulse to turn tail and run.

"I want you to know," Terri said in a faint voice, "that I want us to be friends. I know that you care about me as a person and that's all that matters. I'm not upset with you anymore."

Jesse swallowed. "Uh, sure. That's okay, Terri. Really." He wondered if he was supposed to offer to shake hands with her or anything.

"Well, that's all I wanted to say." She reddened and suddenly ran out of the locker alcove.

Jesse exhaled heavily. "Great," he muttered. Terri had a way of making him feel like one of those rats who beat up on women. What had he ever done except break up with her?

"Uh-hem."

Jesse wheeled about to see Rainey Locklear. She was looking tactful, which told him that she had heard every word that had passed between him and Terri.

"Is this a bad time to talk?" she asked.

"Why would it be a bad time?" growled Jesse. "What do you want, Rainey?"

"I was just wondering if you had ever thought of get-

16

ting rid of your car. I mean, are you about ready to junk it and get something better?"

Jesse stiffened. "Are you saying my car is junk, or what?"

"No offense," said Rainey hastily. "I just want you to keep me in mind if you decide to get rid of it. I could pay you a little if you want—on time. That would save you the trouble of getting it towed."

He turned away. "Too late," he said curtly. "I just sold it to Blake."

"Blake?" She looked stunned. "Blake Farraby?"

"Yes, Blake Farraby. How many Blakes do you know?"

"He bought *your* car?"

"Now, listen here, Rainey—"

"I mean, I was just surprised. I figured him for, well, a different sort of car, that's all."

"He's going to pay me three hundred and fifty."

"Dollars?" asked Rainey incredulously. "He's going to pay you three hundred and fifty dollars?"

Jesse was too annoyed to say another word. He turned abruptly and strode off to his homeroom.

TWO

Second period, Creative Writing—class exercise: Describe how you are different from every other person in this room.

Rainey Locklear

I am one-half Lumbee Indian. My ancestors didn't go in much for signing treaties with the white man, which is why they're not in as bad shape as a lot of other Indians. On the other hand, my mother and I own a beat-up old trailer instead of a big chunk of downtown Raleigh, so that tells you something, too.

My father was an Indian activist. I guess he still is, but I can't be sure because I haven't seen him for some time. He had a misunderstanding with federal marshals over the matter of taking hostages. Papa said it was a publicity gimmick; the Feds said it was kidnapping. My father has been a fugitive now for about three years. I do sometimes get a post card from him, but never with a return address.

Susan Brantley

I am more mature than most of the people my age, particularly the boys. This is not just my imagination. Anyone will tell you it is a biological fact that girls mature faster than boys.

I am ready for a truly romantic, adult relationship, while a lot of the boys my age are still doing gross and stupid things like making rude noises with their armpits. Last year, some guys I know started a mammoth food fight in the cafeteria. I heard it took a week to peel all the food off the walls and the ceiling. I am sorry to say they don't show any sign of being more mature this year.

Blake Farraby

I have visited more foreign countries than most people because my parents like to travel. I have ridden on a camel (bumpy) and an elephant (even worse). I have eaten Italian ice cream (the best) and English cabbage (awful). I realize I am lucky to have had these opportunities, but at the same time, I live under a lot more pressure than most kids. My parents expect me to make top grades at school. I don't know what they would do if I brought home a C. Crack up, probably.

Also, I never know where I am with them. They give me a lot of things, but then, for no reason, just when I get my heart set on something, they'll get all hard-nosed and say I have to learn to do without. They're always telling me I need to learn that life is no picnic. I know one thing already—life with them is no picnic.

Jesse McCracken

I have dead aim. That means I can hit pretty much anything I can see. I've always figured it was something I was born with, kind of like being double-jointed. But last spring I got a new slant on it. Something happened during baseball season that wrecked my concentration and all of a sudden, I couldn't hit a barn with a shoe.

That's when I realized my aim really depends on what's in my head. If I want to hit something, my concentration has to be perfect. For a second I've got to feel like nothing else in the world exists.

Maybe that's why I like baseball. When I'm pitching, everything else fades away and I don't have any problems.

I wish I were out on the field now with the sun on my shoulders and my mind on nothing but the ball.

Ann Lee Smith

People say I am a goody-goody, but that's only because I'm more serious than most people my age. I am interested in nuclear disarmament and other matters that affect the future of our world. Also I always try to do my best at everything I attempt.

Sometimes I get tired of being the responsible one. I would like to do something wild just once, just to see the look on everybody's face. But then I realize that's not the answer for me.

*   *   *

JANICE HARRELL

Michael Dessaseaux

When the moon is full, the hair on the back of my hands begins to grow and my nose takes on a weird shape. Before I know it, I am giving in to the urge to fall down on all fours and run through the neighborhood on silent feet. Yes, dear Mrs. Armstrong, it is true—I am a werewolf. I believe this accounts for my inability to establish a meaningful relationship with a beautiful woman. The thick hair on the back of my hands and my sharp fingernails are a dead giveaway. I trust that plastic surgery will enable me to solve this problem in the near future.

THREE

I can't believe this is my junior year," groaned Susan. She dragged a french fry through the ketchup, held it up, and considered it thoughtfully. "I mean, there has to be some mistake, right? This was the year things were supposed to fall into place for me. This was when it was supposed to get good. Like when I was in the ninth grade, I made this list of everything I wanted by the time I was sixteen—fantastic car, gorgeous boyfriend, strapless black evening dress, white phone in my room. Do you know how many of those things I've got right now?"

"The white phone."

"You've got it. A white phone, and that is absolutely all." Susan popped the dripping french fry into her mouth. "Instead of things getting better and better for me, they are actually getting worse. My life is going down the tubes. And on top of it, our new principal is destroying what miserable shreds of social life we have

23

at this school. I can't believe we have assigned seating at lunch. Do they think we're fourth-graders, or what?''

"It's because of the food fight last year," Ann Lee said.

"No, Ann Lee," said Susan patiently. "Repeat after me—it is because the principal is a creep."

"He used to be principal of a junior high," said Ann Lee. "I think he's having a hard time realizing that high school is different."

"Do you always have to make excuses for people in authority?"

Ann Lee looked down at her plate. "Sorry."

"Blake, tell me the truth, don't you think this assigned seating stuff is awful?" asked Susan.

Blake dropped his tray on the table and sat down.

"Hey, I agree. I could be having fun if I didn't have to sit here with you guys."

"It's not that and you know it," said Susan. "Okay, so it happens that a lot of people we know are in our English class. So what? It's not that I'm crazy to sit anywhere else, it's the principle of the thing. We ought to be able to sit anywhere we want and not just with this one class. At East Gate they get to go off campus for lunch. This guy from over there is telling me this stuff and I'm going, like, unbelievable. It's heaven over there and over here it's Soviet Russia or something. I mean, assigned seating, give me a break!''

Blake flipped his milk carton open. "This is a question for student council, right, Ann Lee?"

Ann Lee looked uncomfortable. "You know we don't have any real power, Blake."

"Maybe you could do something about that," he said. "Lead a revolution or something."

Blake and Susan grinned at each other. Ann Lee's timidity was a standing joke.

"And what about this business of not having any dances?" Susan went on. "Do you realize that even if by some freakish stroke of good luck I actually persuaded my mother to let me have a strapless black evening dress, I wouldn't have a single place to wear it?"

"That's because of the trouble at the fall dance last year. Those kids that got drunk, remember?" said Ann Lee.

"So, a few kids got out of line. Why should the rest of us have our lives ruined just because this school has a criminal element? Are we supposed to quit having fun permanently?"

"Yep," said Blake. "Our principal should get together with my parents. They have the same philosophy of life."

Ann Lee gasped. "Look at Michael. What's he done to himself now?"

Blake glanced over his shoulder. "His bike skidded on the gravel this morning, that's all. He's okay."

Michael limped over to their table. When he fell into a seat, the table shuddered sympathetically. Michael was big. The coaches had tried to persuade him that football was his destiny, but he wasn't interested. He had the tastes of the classic couch potato. Old movies and Fritos were his passions. His clothes tended to look as if he had slept in them, and he was the only boy in the junior class who was going gray.

"If you don't watch out, you're going to kill yourself," Susan told him. "With your reflexes you ought to ride a tricycle—dressed in full armor."

"My darling, I didn't know you cared." He pressed her hand to his lips.

"Please give me my hand back, Michael. I need it to eat with."

Ann Lee frowned. "I wonder if we really laid out some careful plans for a dance, you know, with security arrangements and everything—"

"Don't go to all that trouble on my account." Michael began cutting his meat loaf into tiny squares. He was giving some careful thought to whether he wanted to eat it or just do something disgusting with it.

"It could be a junior-senior dance," Susan said. "Strobe lights and paper leaves. I can see it now. If you get it off the ground, Ann Lee, I'll be chairman of decorations. I think I know where we can get some balloons wholesale. We really *need* this dance. We don't want to be the only class in history that doesn't have anything special to look back on, do we?"

"It's not going to be easy," said Ann Lee. "I think Mr. Bennett heard some pretty wild stories about what happened at the fall dance last year."

"We'll all support you. Won't we, guys?"

"To the death," said Michael.

"Okay, make fun of me," said Susan. "You may not be interested in having a dance, but that doesn't mean the rest of us want to sit around talking about Greta Garbo until we go gray."

"Greta Garbo," said Michael. "Now there was a woman!"

"I hear she was gay," said Blake.

Susan banged her hand on the table, rattling her tray. "Can't we have a serious conversation around here for a change? Honestly, I could sit here and say 'Mickey

Mouse' and somebody would say, 'I hear he was gay.' "

"Funny you should mention that," said Michael. "I've always had my doubts about Mickey."

"Oh, be real, will you?" Susan buried her fingers in her crimped hair.

"You're stuck with us," said Michael. "Assigned seating, remember?"

"Gawd," said Blake. "Look over there."

"Where?" asked Susan.

"Over there. In the big sunglasses. It's Rainey. I think she's coming over."

Sure enough, it was Rainey. With her dark glasses and her long black hair, she could have been a character in one of Michael's favorite old spy movies. She deftly hooked an empty chair from another table and pulled it over to their table.

"What's with the sunglasses?" Blake asked her.

"It's my disguise," Rainey said. She glanced around cautiously. "I don't think anybody saw me come over here. All those people in the lunch line shielded my move."

"But what are you doing over here?" asked Susan.

Rainey took off her sunglasses and sat down. "Escaping from my American history group, naturally. I can't stand eating lunch with them. They never say anything. They just sit there and chew like cows, in rhythm."

"Funny you should mention it. We were just talking about it," said Susan. "This junk about how you have to sit with your class at lunch is awful. Whoever heard of having assigned seating in high school? It's an insult."

"We need to get rid of that new principal," said Rainey.

"What do you have in mind?" asked Michael, looking interested. "Going to take out a contract on him?"

"Don't say something like that to Rainey," said Blake. "She might consider it."

"We shouldn't joke about things like this," said Ann Lee primly. "Crime is no laughing matter. . . ." Remembering then that Rainey's father was a fugitive from justice, she trailed off.

Rainey scarcely noticed Ann Lee's embarrassment. She had been telling the truth when she said she wanted to get away from her classmates in American history, but there was another, more compelling reason she had come to sit at this table. Blake had just snatched away the one car at the school that might possibly be in her price range. She wanted to know why.

She turned to Blake suddenly. "I hear you bought Jesse's car."

"You didn't, Blake!" said Susan. "It's practically the only car in the school that's older than mine."

"It's got a lot of character," said Blake. He had the sensation his face was burning. Sometimes, when Rainey fixed those dark eyes on him, he had the feeling she could read his mind. "The price was right," he added nervously. He knew he needed to change the subject. "Say, Rainey, we're talking about trying to persuade the administration to let us have a dance sometime before Christmas. What do you give for our chances?"

"I'll bet they might let us have a dance if we could absolutely guarantee there wouldn't be any trouble," Ann Lee said. "We could make people show their student I.D.s at the door. And maybe we could hire a couple of off-duty policemen to keep an eye on things."

"That doesn't sound like a dance," said Susan. "It sounds like a minimum-security prison."

"Well, do you want a dance or not?"

All at once they became aware that a man in a three-piece suit stood over them. Looking up in alarm, they saw Mr. Bennett, the principal. Rainey quickly averted her face, hoping she wouldn't be recognized. Surreptitiously, she put her sunglasses back on.

"You have too many chairs at this table," said Mr. Bennett. He had a deep, rasping voice that underscored his authority. "This is a five-chair table. You have six chairs."

Rainey swiftly picked up her tray and dragged the chair she had borrowed from Jesse's table back there.

Satisfied, the principal moved away.

All the boys at Jesse's table stared at Rainey when she sat down. "Hi!" she said with a bright little smile. *It would have to be an all-male table,* she thought. She felt as if she were crashing a locker room.

"So you got run off from the other table," Jesse said. "What happened?"

"Mr. Bennett said we had too many chairs."

"Too many chairs?" he snorted.

"Stupid, isn't it?" Rainey was momentarily stymied. It was certainly bad luck that the principal had shown up. This was a definite setback. She was not going to be a welcome guest at Susan's table if every time she sat down she attracted Mr. Bennett.

"Like I was saying, we've got the talent," the boy sitting next to Jesse declared. "We've got Hayes, and Matthews, and Reddick. But Belleview's real physical, and what I'm saying is we don't need any injuries now, right at the start of the season. They could be real bad news for us."

Jesse spoke in a low voice. "So what were you all talking about over there?"

"Nothing much," said Rainey. "Why?"

He prodded his french fries with his fork. "I just noticed you talking over there, that's all. And I kind of wondered what about."

"Susan and Ann Lee are going to try to get a dance going. I think that was mostly it."

Jesse winced at the burst of laughter from Susan's table. It seemed to him that all the light and color was over at Susan's table and that he was an exile.

"You can't be consistent if you get a lot of injuries," Tony Vipperman said. "That's what our problem was last year. You take some guy like Hayes that's got all fat and out of shape, he's riding for a fall. I don't care how good the guy can pass."

Jesse was looking over Tony's shoulder, gazing at Susan with hungry eyes. Suddenly he stabbed his meat loaf as if he were trying to kill it. In a simpler world, a world without families and dogs and assigned lunchroom seating, he would have gone up to her and said, "Susan, be my woman." Nothing was complicated about this love stuff if you lived in caveman days, he thought. He only wished he had lived back then.

FOUR

_L_ate that afternoon Ann Lee opened the door to Susan's room. "Your mom told me to come on up," she said. "I've been working on the plans for the dance for hours. Want to see what I came up with?"

"Sure." Susan was sprawled on her bed on her stomach, writing in a spiral-bound notebook.

Ann Lee found herself edging around, trying to get in a better position to read what Susan was writing. Why was it she always figured that what Susan was doing was more interesting than anything she was doing? She had been telling herself that if she organized the dance she would be right at the center of things but maybe she had been kidding herself. Susan was the type who could stand on a street corner filing her nails and crowds would gather around to watch. She couldn't compete with that. Very possibly it was a fact of life that Susan was born to the spotlight, while Ann Lee was born to be a member of the chorus. Susan was rocky road ice cream with chocolate sprinkles; Ann Lee was vanilla. Susan was numero uno; Ann Lee was an also-ran. Ann Lee craned her neck and peered at the notebook. "What are you writing?"

"I'm working on my semester project for creative writing. I'm going to write about ordinary things that happen at school. I've even got a title. I'm calling it *Wild Times at West Mount High*." Susan looked at her expectantly. "Don't you see? The title is ironic! I mean, *nothing* interesting, much less wild, ever happens at school."

"Oh," said Ann Lee awkwardly. "So what are you writing about today?"

"I'm making a list of the ten best-looking boys in our class."

In spite of herself, Ann Lee was impressed. Nobody but Susan would dare to turn in something so supremely frivolous.

Sometimes she thought she and Susan had different modes of being, like in those sci-fi stories where people existed in alternative realities. While Ann Lee read the front page and the editorial page of the paper, Susan read the comics and the clothes ads. Ann Lee was sure that if Susan had to name all the justices of the Supreme Court to save her life, she would name only Sandra Day O'Connor and die.

"Limiting it to our class is what made it a challenge," Susan said. "It would have been a lot easier if I had let myself include seniors, but I figured that would be like playing tennis without a net."

Blake was at the top of Susan's list of desirables. Ann Lee noted this fact with regret because Blake was the only boy she felt she could ask, as a friend, to go with her to the dance. That was out if Susan wanted him.

"You left off Jesse McCracken," she pointed out. "Anybody would say he's in the top ten."

Susan shook her head vigorously. "Uh-uh. I don't even think about him, Ann Lee. You know, people like him are different from us. I feel funny about saying it, but it's true."

"I thought you and he had kind of a thing going last year."

Color stained Susan's neck and cheeks. "Not really. Well, we went out some. But then, of course, when his dad shot Muffin . . ."

"Oh, I'm sorry. I forgot. I guess I shouldn't have brought it up."

"It's not that I'm all broken up about Muffin or anything. I mean, we all were shocked, but Muffin was really Daddy's dog. After that time he cornered me on the picnic table and took a bite out of my leg, I was scared to death of him." Susan idly ran her finger along a narrow, jagged white scar on her calf. "It's just—well, what kind of person shoots a dog? Mom and I had a talk about it and I could see it once she pointed it out to me. The McCrackens are different from us, that's all. Jesse's family are the kind of people who drive pickup trucks and eat everything fried in bacon grease. They say 'y'all.' They don't believe in higher education; they sleep with guns under their pillows."

"I never thought Jesse was that different from anybody else."

"I never did myself until Muffin got killed." Susan shivered. "You go around thinking everybody's pretty much the same, but then something like that happens and you realize you're looking at a big difference. Maybe it's the kind of thing that doesn't matter until you start to grow up. I mean, I remember cutting out paper valentines with Jesse in class when we were little, and back then I always liked him. But later on, you start to realize that people's backgrounds matter. You're better off sticking to people who speak your language.''

"So you aren't even putting him on the list?"

"As far as I'm concerned, he doesn't even *exist*."

"But what about Jeff Bass? He's not on there, either."

"Ooo, gross. You think *he* looks good? He looks like Cro-Magnon man, no joke."

"He'd be on my list. He's built."

"Primitive, Ann Lee. You are definitely primitive."

"And I'd cross off Tom Jenkins. He bites his nails. I actually see him playing with the little nail shreds in English. It's revolting."

"When you look like Tom Jenkins, revolting is a new kind of turn-on," said Susan breathily.

Ann Lee giggled. "You are sick."

On the street behind Susan's, at Blake Farraby's house, Jesse McCracken was delivering the car, as promised.

"Great," Blake kept saying over and over as he peeled fifty dollar bills off a roll.

"And here's the title," said Jesse. "All notarized."

"Fantastic," gurgled Blake. "Want me to give you a ride back to your place?"

"My dad'll drive me back," said Jesse. "You sure you don't want to test-drive it?"

"It runs, doesn't it?"

"Sure. I drove it over here."

"It's exactly what I've got in mind. Thanks a lot, Jesse."

Jesse shrugged. "Okay. Good luck with it."

Blake watched Jesse climb into his father's pickup. As the McCrackens drove away, the smile on Blake's face widened.

Blake's mother came down the stairs. "Dear, would you have your friend park on the side of the road? I don't want that car to drip oil on the driveway."

"That's not my friend's car, Mom. It's mine."

"What do you *mean*, it's yours?"

"I bought it." He held up the title and smiled at her. "Signed, sealed, and delivered. Now you won't have to drive me to school anymore."

"How could you possibly buy a car?"

"Remember those bonds Granddad sent me?"

"But he intended those to be saved for your college education!"

"I think Granddad would understand."

"Blake, how much did you pay for that thing?"

"Two hundred," fibbed Blake.

His mother quelled a shudder. "It looks as if it's worth about fifty."

Blake shrugged. "I figured I was lucky to get any car for two hundred."

"I doubt if it's even safe to drive. And where on earth are you going to put it?"

"Well, if you're worried about the oil leaking, I guess the grass would be the best place.

"Park it out front? And then what? Plant geraniums in it? What do you imagine the neighbors are going to think? My God, Blake, that's the kind of thing that brings down property values. We'll be getting letters from people's lawyers next."

"It was what I could afford," said Blake with an air

of conscious virtue. "I had to be sure to save out enough for insurance and gas and things like that."

Mrs. Farraby held her hand to her forehead. "Look, this is giving me a headache. Your father is going to have to talk to you about it when he gets in."

Susan just happened to be looking out the window when the McCrackens' pickup passed her house. "That's Jesse now in that truck," she gasped.

Ann Lee rushed to the window. "You don't think they're going to shoot at the house, do you?"

"Of course not." Susan laughed a little shakily.

The two girls watched as the truck took the corner. Four floodlights were mounted on its cab for night hunting, but other than that it was unremarkable.

"What can they be doing out here?" Susan stared at Ann Lee. "They live way out on the edge of town."

"I'll bet it's about Jesse's car! Don't you remember Blake telling us he bought it?"

"I hope Mom didn't look out and recognize the truck. If she tells Dad, he'll have a heart attack. He still can't talk about Muffin without falling to pieces. I mean, he would have an apoplectic fit if he even saw them."

Jesse and his dad drove directly to a car dealership. There Jesse put Blake's payment together with his summer earnings and bought a "previously owned" sporty red Camaro. He drove off in it feeling considerably lighter of heart than he had in months.

What made him feel better, he realized, was not just the Camaro, but writing a love letter to Susan. Creative writing class had shown him that putting his feelings down on paper could release some of the pressure he was feeling inside. He had written a draft of the letter the night before. He didn't intend to sign his name to it, of course.

As he drove down Sunset, he reached around and felt for it in his hip pocket. It wasn't there. He blanched. No, wait a minute, calm down, he told himself—it wasn't addressed, and it wasn't signed. Maybe it was kind of embarrassing to think that somebody at the car dealership might pick it up and read it, but nobody could possibly connect it to him. And he sure wasn't going to go back to look for it. No way. He would just write another one later.

The next day he was going to slip the letter through a ventilation slot in Susan's locker. Just thinking about it cheered him up. He turned the Camaro's radio on very loud and smiled.

*S*econd period, Creative Writing—class exercise: Describe your school.

Jesse McCracken

Wet paper towels stuck to the bathroom floor, tired dribbles of water leaking out of the water fountains, the smell of dirty sneakers—that's what I think of when I think of school. When I get home I always want to change my clothes, like maybe the smell of the place has stuck to me or something. Most of the time school is okay, but when I get away I don't want to be reminded of it.

Ann Lee Smith

West Mount High School is made up of a series of plain brick buildings dating from 1960. On the average forty percent of its three thousand students go on to college. Graduates of West Mount contribute to our community in many different ways.

Rainey Locklear

At this school they act as if everything's cut and dried. If you don't give the answer the teacher has in the answer book, then you're wrong and you can forget arguing about it. In real life, it's having a brain that counts, but in school what counts is the answer book. I ask you, did Einstein have an answer book? Did Newton?

I would say that the hidden plan behind this emphasis on the answer book is to turn out kids who all think exactly alike. Luckily, in my case it's not working.

Michael Dessaseaux

I know we complain about this school, but has anyone ever looked at it from the school's point of view? In a recent interview, our school had this to say—

Please don't put paper towels in the toilets, don't throw mashed potatoes on the ceiling of the lunchroom, and give a little thought to how *you* would feel with chewing gum stuck to your face.

As to the work, the hours are good and I can't complain about the vacation, but the social life stinks. Except for a brief and meaningless fling with a classroom trailer, I can't remember when I last got kissed.

Blake Farraby

This is an okay place to go to school but it's sort

of cliquey. People run around with their own little crowd—the artsy kids, the hackers, the skaters, the nerds, the in-crowd, the deadheads. I think people can miss out on a lot that way, but I guess I'm as bad as anybody. You can get pretty comfortable in your own little rut.

Susan Brantley

School is where I pass the time while I wait for my life to happen.

Susan stared at the single sentence on her notebook paper. She couldn't think of a single additional word to write.

She was wearing five brass bracelets and six silver ones, plus earrings made of dangling gold coins, four neck chains, and two chain belts. This ensemble was topped off with a jeans jacket with brass studs and buckled pockets. Every time she moved she could hear herself go *chink-chink*. When she had dressed that morning, going heavy metal was the only way she could think of to add interest to her life.

The bell rang and Susan jumped up right away, clanging wildly. She tossed her paper on Mrs. Armstrong's desk.

"Only one sentence?" Mrs. Armstrong raised her eyebrows.

"I have writer's block." Susan hurried out of the classroom. She always ran out of Mrs. Armstrong's class because she didn't want to risk bumping into Jesse at the door.

Michael caught up with her. "Don't tell me, let me guess. You're disguised as a tambourine."

"You've got it." Susan shimmied a little and grinned.

A second later kids poured into the halls. Susan let the traffic carry her along until she reached the end of A wing, then stepped into the locker alcove.

Michael's locker door banged open behind her. "Don't you ever wonder what everybody else is writing in that class?" he asked. "I keep getting up to sharpen my pencil so I can read over everybody's shoulder."

"You are weird, Michael." She pulled out her trig book and an envelope fluttered to her feet. It had her name on it. Funny. Somebody must have stuck it in through the ventilation slits in her locker. She picked it up and tore it open.

I think of you all the time—of your softness, your beauty. You are the melody in my heart. All day and all night my blood sings Susan, Susan.

Susan gulped and darted a quick look behind her. Could Michael have written this? Was he standing by fiddling with his books just so he could watch her reaction? No, no, get real, she told herself. Just because he's here now doesn't mean he put it there.

Michael stuffed a few sheets of notebook paper into his trig book. "You aren't even a little bit curious?"

Susan blinked at him. "What?"

He waved a hand in front of her face. "Are you in a trance or something? Hey, what's that you've got there?"

"Nothing," she gulped. "I've got to run. Bye."

Her heart pounded as she hurried to chemistry class. Could the letter be some kind of joke? Michael's sense of humor was pretty unpredictable. She sneaked the letter out of her trig book and read it over again. It didn't sound like a joke. It didn't sound like Michael, either. And the handwriting was all wrong. Michael was left-handed and his letters slanted in the other direction. Okay, it wasn't Michael. Then who was it?

As soon as Susan got home from school, she got Ann Lee to come over. She needed to show the letter to someone who was absolutely sane, impartial, and reliable.

" 'My blood sings Susan, Susan'?" Ann Lee raised her eyebrows.

"Tell me the truth. Do you think it sounds like something a crazy person would write? You know, like those creeps who stalk the girl in horror movies?"

"But didn't you say it was in your locker? It has to be somebody you know. At least somebody who knows which locker is yours."

"You're right! I knew you'd say something sensible like that. I feel a lot better already. After all, I don't know any psychotic creeps, do I?"

"I don't think so. Actually, I think the note's kind of sweet."

"But why doesn't whoever it is just come out and tell me he likes me?"

"He's not going to tell you to your face that you are the melody in his heart, is he? Nobody talks like that."

"Right! I hadn't thought of that." Susan suddenly felt breathless. "Tell me the truth, Ann Lee, do you think it could be from some senior?"

"Can you think of any senior boys who know your locker number?"

"I guess not," Susan said reluctantly. The seniors had lockers in conveniently located alcoves, not out at the ends of the wings, where the sophomore and junior lockers were. She had to admit that a senior wouldn't have had much chance to see her at her locker.

"I wish somebody would send *me* a love letter." Ann Lee sighed.

"Don't worry. The chances are that it's from some dork."

"Not necessarily. It could be from somebody like Cyrano de Bergerac. He was dashing and romantic, and had a beautiful soul, but he didn't court Roxanne in person because he was afraid she'd laugh at his big nose."

"I think I saw the movie. Steve Martin was in it, right?"

"Not exactly. I believe Cyrano lived in the seventeenth century. Edmond Rostand did a play about him."

"Same idea, anyway. But the thing is, I don't know anybody with that big a nose."

"That's just an example. It could be somebody who's just shy."

Susan frowned. "I just wish I knew who."

The light from the television flickered on Mrs. Lock-lear's round face as she soaked her feet in hot water and Epsom's salts. She stirred restlessly. "Rainey, hon, will you hand me a glass of ice water?"

A picture of Rainey as a baby sat on the white cro-cheted dresser scarf that topped the television set. In the picture, Rainey had wide serious eyes and was holding a rubber duck. Beside the baby picture was a silver spoon that said *Souvenir of Asheville* and a white mug with *Mom* written on it in gilt letters. On the other side was a black plastic ashtray marked Carolina Bar and Grill. The Car-olina Bar and Grill was where Rainey's mother worked as a waitress.

Rainey put a glass of ice water on the end table next to her mother and cast a doubtful look around her. The Sunday comics still lay folded on the table next to a large bottle of aspirin. Over the orange- and green-flowered couch was a picture made of seashells. The place did not, she decided, look like much.

She raised her voice over the commercial. "Mom, if I had a car, I could get a job after school."

"That would be nice, hon, but cars cost money. We just can't manage it right now. It cost so much just to have the trailer towed over here."

During the summer, the board of health had condemned the Magnolia Trailer Park's well and the owner had decided to close down rather than bring the water up to standard. So Rainey's mom had had to pay a trucker what seemed like a small fortune to cart their old trailer from the Magnolia Trailer Park to the new Starlight Trailer Park. The move had jerked the trailer out of alignment and ever since then the kitchen cabinets refused to close properly and the window in the living room wouldn't open.

"I'm going to keep my eye out," said Rainey. "Maybe I can find a bargain."

"It'd have to be free, so don't get your hopes up." Mrs. Locklear groaned softly. "Hon, would you go get the clothes off the line? I bet I'm getting fallen arches. I feel like a truck ran over my feet."

Rainey went out to the clothesline behind the trailer. Outside the moon was like a searchlight and beyond the cement paving the ground was damp with dew. She could smell the faint rank scent of weeds crushed under her shoes. One of the McCrackens' hounds heard her moving around and howled. The other hounds joined in, and the

45

dogs of the trailer park started yipping in concert. The line-dried clothes, only slightly damp from the dew, felt stiff as she pulled them off the line. Suddenly the Mc-Crackens' dogs fell silent. The trailer park dogs kept on yipping, but with less conviction. Rainey looked across the road and spotted Jesse passing in front of a lighted window of his house. He must have been the one who shut the hounds up. He seemed to be carrying something bulky under his arm.

She watched him go into his backyard. The moonlight on his pale jacket made him easy to follow. Near a bush he bent to unroll the package under his arm. When he got down and then disappeared from her view, it slowly dawned on her that what he had been carrying was a sleeping bag. He was going to bed down outside. Talk about a fresh-air fiend—this was ridiculous. She didn't see how he could sleep with that bright moon in his face.

She took the clothes inside and dumped them on the couch. She moved quietly because her mother had fallen asleep in front of the television. Mrs. Locklear's face was shiny with fatigue and her feet looked pathetically white in the pot of tepid water. Rainey knew if she turned off the television her mother would wake up, so she slipped into her room and got dressed for bed, accompanied by the sound of the eleven o'clock news. Moonlight streamed through the ruffled curtains and glittered on the mylar Happy Birthday balloon tied to her bedpost.

Once she got on her nightgown, she climbed up on her bed and looked out the window. It was strange to think that Jesse was lying out there staring at the same moon she was. The narrow dirt road that separated his yard from the trailer park might as well be an ocean for all they had to do with each other. She couldn't figure him

46

out. At first she had thought that with them living right across the street from each other she would get to know him better. But he never spoke to her, never stopped to pass the time of day. Like the old farmhouse he lived in, he stood a bit apart from the people in the trailer park. There was nothing neighborly about him. It was as if he thought he was better than they were.

On the other side of the dirt road, Jesse could feel the chill in the night air. He pulled his sleeping bag up to his chin and stared at the moon. Blue's breath ruffled his hair. *Phoomph, phoomph, whiffle* went the dog. "Roll over, Blue," he muttered. "You're snoring." Blue normally slept inside the house, but when Jesse took his sleeping bag outside, Blue had insisted on going along. The other dogs were gathered around the sleeping bag, too, but Blue had the place of honor at Jesse's head. Jesse shoved him gently. The hound shifted his position slightly, then began snoring once more. Jesse sighed. He wondered if Susan had gotten his letter yet. He would have given a lot to know what she had thought of it. Sometimes she seemed a million miles away from him. He liked to think she was looking at the night sky right then, the way he was, feeling small in comparison to all those faraway stars and trying, like him, to feel that the problem of human beings were not so important in the big scheme of things.

He wasn't sleepy at all. Already, another letter to Susan was taking shape in his head. "Dearest Susan, my heart's light—" He put his hands behind his head and smiled up at the sky. It was a good beginning.

Six

Susan found Jesse's second letter in her locker the following week.

Dearest Susan, my heart's light, how I long to be near you. I think sometimes that you are my best self. Does that make you laugh a little? Go ahead and laugh. It won't hurt my feelings. I love to see you laugh. I even like the way you tear onion rings apart to eat the inside—my love, my life, my funny Susan.

When Susan got to chemistry class she nudged Ann Lee. "I got another one."

"Another what?"

"Another _letter_." She pushed it across the table for Ann Lee to read.

"Class, would you please get out pencil and paper," said Mr. Finch.

"A pop quiz," Susan groaned. "What next? Is this my life or a black comedy or something?" She pulled out her notebook. At least she had to admit her life had suddenly gotten more interesting. Whenever she thought about the love letter, she felt deliciously sick with excitement.

After chemistry Ann Lee gave her back the letter. "It sounds like somebody who knows you pretty well. He's seen you destroy an order of onion rings, right? It almost has to be somebody you've been out with."

"But I've been out with so many guys," said Susan.

Ann Lee had to concentrate so hard on not looking jealous that her powers of analytic thought were temporarily impaired. It was Susan who pointed out the problem. "And if it's somebody I've been out with, and if they feel that way about me, why don't they ask me out again and tell me so?"

Ann Lee was hesitant. "It could be somebody that you parted with on bad terms."

"Like Tommy Leonard, you mean? I told him I never wanted to see him again after the way he kept pawing me at the drama club awards banquet. Talk about mortifying! If it turns out to be Tommy Leonard, Ann Lee, I am going to be *so* disappointed."

"What about Jesse?"

"You must be kidding. 'My heart's light,' Jesse? He would never say that."

"I know it's hard to picture, but it's hard to picture anybody saying this kind of thing. Maybe love letters are just different. Maybe they don't sound the way people talk."

"Besides, Jesse hates me. You know my dad fixed it so they built that awful trailer park right across from his house to get back at them about what happened to Muffin. Every time I catch him looking at me, Ann Lee, it gives me chills. He *stares* at me in this way that just has to be called threatening." Susan tossed her chemistry book in her locker. "You would think that whoever wrote them would want to give me a clue, at least. I mean, what's the use of writing these letters if I don't know who did it? What's the good of them?"

"Maybe the onion rings are the first clue. Maybe there'll be other clues later."

"My heart's light." Susan's voice grew soft. "Well, it does sound kind of sweet, doesn't it?"

Saturday was Blake's birthday. His parents had a back-yard barbecue in honor of the occasion. A company called Balloon Bonanza had constructed an archway of balloons over the swimming pool.

"Kind of looks like a supermarket opening, doesn't it?" said Blake.

Michael regarded the balloons thoughtfully. "No. Not quite big enough. Gala opening of a dentist's office, maybe."

Blake's hands were thrust in his pockets, aching for keys to jangle. He stared anxiously at the balloons. He hoped they weren't going to be his only surprise.

"I love succotash," Michael said, his mouth full.

The backyard was full of neighbors and friends of Blake's parents. His mother waltzed by and handed him a plate. "We don't want the birthday boy to pass out from hunger, do we? Remember to save room for the cake, boys."

"Marguerite!" A portly gray-haired man hailed Mrs. Farraby. "Is that Blake's car out front?"

She winced a little. "Yes, he bought it with his own money. Blake has always been *so* independent." With her chin held high, she sailed toward the bar.

Blake gloomily eyed a forkful of chopped pork. He wasn't crazy about barbecue, actually, but nobody had asked for his opinion.

Susan and Ann Lee brought their plates over to the chairs by the pool. "Those balloons are fantastic," Susan said. "I mean, it's like a balloon rainbow. I love it. You're so lucky. My mother's idea of party decorations is a pin-the-tail-on-the-donkey poster or something. We never have big parties."

Blake was beginning to suspect that his parents had called his bluff on the car, and the idea gave him a faintly sick feeling. He had hoped to find keys to a new car on his breakfast plate that morning, but all he'd found was eggs and bacon. Then he had hoped a salesman would come driving up just before the party with his car while a wrecker towed off the old heap in the front yard. He had reasoned that his parents would never invite three hundred friends to their house and let them be greeted by the sight of Jesse's car. But he had been wrong.

Now time was running out. There wasn't much of his birthday left. He wished he had got a mechanic to check out Jesse's car before he had shelled out three hundred and fifty hard-to-get dollars. What was it going to be like to drive that old car? Sure, it was better than no car at all, but not *that* much better. Of course, he could paint slogans on it and make it a kind of joke, but he was afraid that might hurt Jesse's feelings. It looked as if he might have to drive it and look proud of it. He felt a sharp pain in his gut that he didn't think was caused by the barbecue. Acute disappointment, probably.

"You sure don't look very happy," said Susan, "for somebody who's having a birthday."

"The man's coming face to face with his own mortality," said Michael. "What do you expect?"

"When do you take the driver's test?" asked Ann Lee.

"Pretty soon, I guess."

"You ought to go out of town to take it," said Susan. "The examiners here are so tough. Like I got marked off for not coming to a full stop, and I *had* come to a full stop, and they were so picky about the parallel parking you wouldn't believe it. I only knocked over one little post and you would have thought I murdered somebody."

Blake closed his eyes. "I can parallel park."

"Yeah, not all of us have to take the test twice," said Michael.

"Don't give me a hard time, Michael. You can't even drive that stupid motorcycle of yours."

"Hey, you're speaking of the machine I love."

"Are you sick, Blake?" asked Ann Lee. "I could get you an aspirin."

Blake shook his head. He actually felt physically ill from disappointment. That could happen, he knew. The power of the mind over the body was the whole basis of the way voodoo worked in Haiti. When his parents had to watch him pine away and die, they would be sorry for not getting him a decent car.

"Barbecue is my favorite food in the entire world," said Michael. "Of course, it's got to be cooked right and this is cooked right—finely chopped, delicately spiced, very hot."

"What I like to eat," said Susan, "is boiled shrimp, watermelon, and fried onion rings."

Blake made a valiant stab at keeping up his end of the conversation. "You don't eat onion rings, Susan—you destroy them." He smiled weakly.

Susan and Ann Lee exchanged a quick glance.

"I know everybody's not finished," yelled Dr. Farraby, "but we're going to go ahead with the birthday cake now."

The caterers rolled out an immense cake in three tiers and lit the sixteen candles on top. Mrs. Farraby took Blake's arm and dragged him over to the cake. People began singing "Happy Birthday."

When Blake sucked in a breath and blew at the candles, three were left burning. The caterer's man tactfully finished them off.

So I don't get my wish, thought Blake. *But then I knew that already.*

A horn sounded and the crowd east of the swimming pool started to part. They pulled way back to make room for a tomato-red Corvette. Blake felt dizzy as the car drove into the backyard accompanied by a burst of applause.

"Boy, you are so lu-cky!" said Susan.

Blake was ready to weep. Dr. Farraby put his arm around him and squeezed.

"You're setting a bad example, R.J.!" somebody called out of the crowd. "We're all going to suffer for this."

Dr. Farraby looked embarrassed. "Well, I figure they're only young once."

Blake's mother sidled up to them. "Now, young man," she said playfully, "I want that heap out of the front yard at once, you hear?"

"Yes, ma'am. I'll take care of it." He supposed there

54

must be wreckers who carried heaps away to automobile graveyards. But if he did that, what would he tell Jesse? He ran his hand lightly and lovingly over the smooth red finish of the Corvette's hood and decided he'd worry about all that later.

"Want some birthday cake?" asked his mother.

Blake shook his head. He had a lump in his throat and wasn't sure he could swallow.

The next afternoon Blake took the driving test and made an almost perfect score. The examiner shook his hand and congratulated him. There was nothing stopping him from driving his car to school now. Thinking about it he felt almost drunk with excitement. He admitted to himself that half the fun of the car would be showing it off.

In the morning the only down note was provided by the memo his mother had left beside his plate when she left for an early beauty shop appointment. "Blake— Don't forget you promised me you'd get rid of that heap out front *immediately*."

Blake put that problem aside for the moment. He wanted to savor the idea of his new car. After breakfast, when he slid behind the wheel of the Corvette, he breathed deeply of the smell of factory-fresh plastic and decided this was as good as it got. The gleaming tomato-colored hood stretched out before him like a promise of infinite happiness.

It seemed all wrong to take his powerful car to school. The Corvette was made for the open road, for blue skies, for hot-and-cold-running blondes, not school. The only trouble was, if he gave the car its head and took off for the beach, he knew his father would make sure he didn't have it for long. Resigned, he sighed and drove on toward Baker Street. Soon, the Corvette pulled up to join the slow-moving line of cars that led onto the school grounds.

"Je-rusalem, Blake! This thing yours?" Roan Martin had hopped out of his car.

Blake winced. "Hey, don't leave your fingerprints on it."

"Yes, your excellency! Excuse me, sir!"

"I mean, I just got it, you know?" Horns blared. "Watch it! The line's starting to move again."

Blake was relieved to see Roan get back in his own car. Heaven only knew what the oil off people's fingers would do to his finish. He wasn't crazy about driving his new car into the school parking lot, now that he thought about it. What if somebody like Susan sideswiped him? He remembered her saying she had barely passed the driving test. Somebody like that was a hazard. His personal opinion was that they ought to make the driving test stiffer and keep people like her off the road.

A teacher's whistle blew and directed Blake's lane into the parking lot. For a moment he was tempted to straddle two parking spaces to give his car extra space on each side but he quickly reconsidered. With parking in such short supply, if he hogged an extra space, he could get rammed by an irate student.

He chose a space close to the administration building. Cars quickly pulled in on either side of him with what seemed wanton recklessness, but at least neither of them scraped any of his paint. He wiped his forehead with his handkerchief.

Rainey, coming from the direction of the bus lot, was stopped in her tracks by the sight of the Corvette. "Blake!" she cried. "It's beautiful."

He got out of it, blushing. "Birthday present," he mumbled.

"What are you going to do with your old car, now?"

"I don't know. I've got to get rid of it somehow, I guess."

"I might be able to take it off your hands." Her voice was carefully casual.

"That'd be great, Rainey."

"I know it's in awful shape. I just thought I'd offer to take it off your hands."

For a second Blake wondered if she was hinting around that she expected him to pay her for taking it away. He hoped not. He had already overextended himself buying it in the first place.

The bell sounded like an explosion near them and Rainey turned to go.

"Well, come over and take a look at it anyway!" Blake said as she moved away.

A loud roar behind him signaled that Michael had arrived. "Watch where you're going, you idiot! You nearly hit me," yelled a rasping voice. Blake wheeled around and saw the principal dusting his pants off with his hands. His face was purple and he looked as if he were about to explode. Blake supposed he had been patrolling the parking lot looking for unstickered cars when Michael's bike had knocked him down. Michael parked and charged past Blake, still wearing his helmet. "Young man!" Mr. Bennett bellowed. "You stop right there!"

A minute later Michael collided with Rainey in the hall of A wing. "Out of my way," he panted. "I'm a fugitive."

"What did you do?"

"Nearly flattened Mr. Bennett. I don't think he recognized me, though."

Shauna Greenberg put her hand lightly on Rainey's arm to get her attention. Rainey could see Shauna's lips moving, but over all the noise in the hall she couldn't make out the girl's gentle voice. "What?"

"I said thanks for the tip," Shauna repeated. "I really do like Mrs. Morris's class a lot better. My mother told them it was a personality conflict, just like you said, and they moved me the very next day."

"Glad to help out." Rainey felt that things were going her way at last. She knew in her bones that she was going to be able to make an advantageous deal with Blake about the car. After all, he had practically begged her to buy it, hadn't he?

At lunchtime she observed that she was by no means the only person who had been affected by the arrival of Blake's Corvette. Susan was obviously impressed. How else could you account for the way she was practically licking her lips at the sight of Blake?

'Blake, that car is just so cool," Susan said. "I mean, how does it feel to be driving it? Can I touch you?"

'You can touch me. Just don't touch my car."

Susan's finger rested delicately on his shirt. "Ssst! Oh, he's hot!" She pulled her finger away quickly and laughed.

Blake watched Michael approach with relief. With three girls and one guy, a fellow could feel a little outnumbered, particularly when one of the girls was Susan, who was not, let's face it, one of the low-key personalities of all time.

Michael threw himself into a chair. "I have survived the Inquisition. I have lived to tell the tale."

"I heard them calling your name on the intercom," Ann Lee said. "What happened?"

"Well, friends, this morning in my haste to further my education and eager for knowledge, as usual, I rode up pretty fast and almost hit Mr. Bennett."

"You should have gone ahead and run over him," said Rainey.

"What can I say?" Michael shrugged. "I missed."

"I can't believe you had the nerve to just run away like you did," said Blake. "I saw you taking off. What'd he do when he caught up with you?"

"I am about to tell you," said Michael. "If you'd just shut up."

Ann Lee was already getting anxious about the prospect of speaking to Mr. Bennett about the dance. "Did he scream at you a lot?"

"Some," said Michael modestly. "But I didn't break down."

"How did he know it was you?" asked Susan. "I've seen you coming up to school. Your own mother wouldn't know you in that helmet."

"He checked the registration number of the parking sticker," said Rainey.

"Is that how he did it?" Michael looked at Rainey admiringly. "I was kind of wondering."

"Rainey thinks of everything," said Blake.

"He was going to throw the book at me," Michael said. "He even mentioned ripping up my parking permit! Yes, you may well look shocked. I was horrified."

"So how did you get out of it?"

"First I apologized all over the place, sort of abased myself thoroughly, told him I had a lot of personal problems at home that I wasn't at liberty to discuss and I guessed it was affecting my concentration.''

"Don't you have any pride, man?" said Blake.

"Actually, no. The only thing is, now I've got to go see the counselor." Gloom momentarily crossed Michael's face. "I just have to keep telling myself it's better than losing my parking permit."

Susan squeezed ketchup on her plate and looked at Rainey thoughtfully. "Mr. Bennett hasn't been near us since that time you had to move. Why? What have you done, Rainey?"

"Nothing. This is a five-person table and there are five people at it," Rainey said smugly.

"Hey, that's right. I hadn't thought about it." Susan looked around. "Well, what happened to Shauna? I can't remember when she was here last. She never said much so I didn't exactly notice when she quit being around."

"Her class schedule changed and now she has second lunch."

"How could her schedule change so late in the semester?"

"Personality conflict."

"Oh."

Rainey smiled enigmatically and buttered her bun.

One table over, Jesse was watching Susan with a sour taste in his mouth. He had seen her put her finger against Blake's chest and look into his eyes. She was coming on to him, all right. He could hardly believe that she could be so dazzled by a fancy red car, but what other explanation was there? She hadn't been all over Blake last week before he got the car, had she? It was disgusting. How materialistic could you get?

"Did you see that Corvette of Blake's?" Tony Vipperman asked.

"Did I see it!" Vince Marlow choked. "I drooled all over it. Jeez, it must be nice to be rich."

"Two hundred and forty-five horsepower," said Tony. "That sucker'll go from zero to sixty in five and a half seconds."

"Isn't that about as good as a Porsche?"

"Better. The nine eleven Cabriolet only has two hundred fourteen h.p."

"Just remind me not to get into a race with Farraby, that's all."

"He'll probably just use it for getting back and forth from the library."

"What a waste."

"A waste? Hey, it's criminal. Would I love to get that baby on the open road."

A fantasy started to form in Jesse's mind—he and Blake out on the old airport road; an excited crowd gathered, hungry for blood. Susan, of course, would be crying and begging them not to drag, but he and Blake, faces grim, would climb slowly into their cars. "Gentlemen," someone would say. "Start your engines." Or something like that. Jesse had never actually seen a drag race except in the movies. Then with a roar they would take off. By cunning and superior driving skill, Jesse would easily pull his elderly Camaro ahead of the more powerful Corvette. And then Blake would run off the road and his car would burst into flames. Perfect.

Jesse realized he was smiling idiotically. He was going to have to pull himself together and concentrate on eating his hamburger if he didn't want people to think he had flipped out. The actual fact of the matter was that even if he were crazy enough to risk his license in a race, he couldn't picture Blake going along with it. He couldn't even picture Blake getting mad. Blake was not the kind of person who felt very strongly about anything. He was just kind of—bland. Jesse shot a burning look at Susan. How *could* she?

*R*ainey was relieved to learn that she could catch a
city bus to Blake's neighborhood. It did make sense, of
course, that all the people who worked as maids out in
those fancy neighborhoods had to get there somehow.
She was afraid to wait until Saturday morning when her
mother could drive her over to look at the car. Someone
else might snap it up before then. She had already lost it
once and couldn't take the chance of losing it again. She
discovered she could easily walk the few blocks from the
bus stop on Beal Street over to Amaryllis Street where
Blake lived.

The next afternoon she caught the bus at a stop two
blocks from school. The bus didn't go out where she
lived, and she wasn't sure how she'd get home if she and
Blake couldn't come to terms on the car, but she pushed
that thought out of her mind. She had to make sure Blake
did sell her the car.

When Rainey got on the bus, one other person was

already on it—a black woman who looked as if her feet hurt and who reminded Rainey of her mother. The bus drove down Sunset Avenue, then turned off into the affluent neighborhoods of the west city.

After a while the bus driver took a toothpick out of his mouth and spoke. "Beal Street."

With a sighing noise, the folding doors opened. Rainey thanked the bus driver and got off the bus very quickly. She had an unreasonable fear of the folding doors. It seemed to her they were snapping at her, trying to snare an arm or leg. What if someday she was a trifle slow and they succeeded in trapping her arm? She could easily imagine herself trotting along outside, trying to get the attention of the bus driver while he drove on, oblivious, chewing on his toothpick.

The lawns in Blake's neighborhood were vast and the neighborhood was oddly quiet. Rainey might have thought a neutron bomb had wiped out the entire population except that men from a lawn service were busily raking and edging in front of an impressive-looking house.

When she got to Amaryllis Street, she spotted Blake's house at once since Jesse's heap was parked in front of it. The door of the big house flew open and Blake trotted out to meet her.

He looked at her anxiously. "So, what do you think?"

She peered in a car window, wondering if she should kick the tires.

"I probably ought to tell you," Blake said, "that it really has more than twenty thousand miles on it. I think the odometer has flipped over."

"You mean it really has a hundred and twenty thousand miles?"

He cleared his throat. "Or maybe two hundred."

"I see."

"Do you want to test-drive it? I've got the keys right here, but you've got to get in on the other side because this door doesn't exactly work. You do have your license, don't you?"

"I got it after driver's ed this summer." She walked around the car. She started to kick a tire but thought better of it. What would she do if something fell off?

"Nothing fancy." Blake eyed her uneasily. "But it is transportation."

"It's got some rust."

"I guess you've got to expect that on a car this old. It's not rusted all the way through, though."

Rainey decided to come to the point immediately. "I can't afford to pay you very much."

"How much?"

"A hundred."

"Aw, gee, I paid Jesse three-fifty." Rainey pawed the ground with the toe of her shoe. "Yeah, but maybe you needed it more, uh, urgently than I do."

Suddenly Blake felt sure Rainey saw through his plot to shame his parents into buying him a car, and his ears felt warm. "A hundred would be okay, I guess."

"But I'd have to pay you on time. I mean, I could pay you ten dollars a month until it was all paid off."

Blake saw his mother's station wagon turning into the driveway. She was home early from shopping.

"Sold!" Blake cried. He slapped the keys into Rainey's palm. "Take it now and I'll give you the title later this week, okay?"

"Okay." Rainey got in the car on the other side and

65

scooted across the seat. What a great feeling it was to be behind the wheel! The car coughed as she started it up, but to her relief, when she put it in gear, it began to move.

"Good luck!" Blake said heartily. He patted the car gently, as if he, too, was afraid something would fall off.

Rainey's new purchase was not exactly like the car she had driven in driver's education and she had to concentrate very carefully on what she was doing. She drove slowly down Amaryllis Street, and caught sight of her happy face in the rearview mirror. It was so weird to think that now she could go anywhere she wanted. She glanced at the gas gauge. Well, almost anywhere, anyway.

Once she got the car home she began cleaning it. Grit was wedged in the exposed layers of plastic and metal where the floor had gotten badly worn. After a few minutes' work with a whiskbroom, she understood why it was so dirty—it was almost impossible to clean. She gave up on sweeping and instead began digging gum wrappers out from between the seat cushions. Groping around the seat belt on the driver's side, her fingers felt a stiff piece of paper. She fished it out and unfolded it.

I think of you all the time—of your softness, your beauty. You are the melody in my heart. All day and all night my blood sings nothing but Susan, Susan.

Rainey blinked. Good grief! *You are the melody in my heart?* How phony-sounding can you get? She couldn't imagine Blake coming out with this kind of bilge and it lowered her opinion of him considerably to read it.

Susan was Susan Brantley, of course. All the boys seemed to like her. Rainey laid the note neatly on top of the little pile of gum papers she was making on the back seat. The more she thought about it, the more she realized that Blake and Susan were as obvious a pairing as Barnum and Bailey or peanut butter and jelly. She should have seen it before.

Feeling slightly depressed, she began sweeping off the front seat.

"Hey, that's my car!"

Jesse's voice startled Rainey so much that she bumped her head.

She rubbed her forehead. "It's not your car anymore. I bought it from Blake. Now that he's got the Corvette, he doesn't need it."

"Oh, yeah, the Corvette. I noticed. How much did you give him?"

"A hundred."

"He gave it to you for a hundred?" Jesse snorted. "He must be sweet on you."

"Don't be stupid." She backed awkwardly out of the car.

"Well, you got a good deal. It may not look like much, but I practically rebuilt it from the engine out."

Jesse lifted the hood. "You better go get the hose. The radiator leaks a little bit."

Rainey went inside and got a quart jar of water for the car. She watched as Jesse took off the radiator cap because she wanted to be able to remember how to do it.

"Be careful you don't do this when the engine is hot," he said, "or that antifreeze will spout right up in your eyes and blind you permanently."

Rainey gulped. She didn't know when she would be

able to summon the nerve to get near the radiator after hearing that. "Is that all the water it needs? It looks like you just poured in a little bit."

"Yeah, well, I guess it isn't leaking as bad as I thought."

She was very glad to hear it. She was also pleased to see Jesse taking an interest in his old car. He might prove very useful if the car had mechanical difficulties in the future.

After he left, she gathered up the handful of gum wrappers in the backseat. *Wait a minute,* she thought. *What about the letter?* She carefully checked the floor of the back seat, then ran her fingers between the cushions of the back seat. No sign of it. She stood up and shot a speculative look at Jesse's house. He had been very stupid to take the letter and not the gum wrappers. If he had taken the gum wrappers, she would have figured he was only helping clean up. But since it was just the letter that was missing—well, she figured she knew who it was now who was so crazy about Susan. It had not been Blake who lost that letter in the car at all, but Jesse!

_____ *EIGHT*

Second period, Creative Writing—class exercise:
Describe a moral dilemma you have faced recently
and tell how you resolved it.

Rainey Locklear
   I found an anonymous love letter, and I am pretty
sure I know who wrote it. The girl it was written to
thinks that the boy who wrote it hates her. But *au
contraire,* as we say in French—he is disgustingly
crazy about her. Should I let the girl know about the
letter?
   My dilemma is complicated by the fact that I don't
want to tick the boy off in any way, as he may be
able to help me keep my old car running. And if he
wanted the girl to know who wrote the letter, he
would have signed it, right? Also I don't know
if he actually sent the letter. It is barely possible that
he was working on his creative writing project, ti-

tled, perhaps, "Hypothetical Love Letters." Also, it is possible that I am wrong both about who wrote it and who it was written to. Though I am very rarely wrong, it is a possibility.

I am happy to say that after much thought about this moral dilemma, I decided to do the right thing. Since the letter was not intended for my eyes the right thing to do is to act as if I have not seen it. This course of action also happens to be in my own best interests.

Blake Farraby

I faced a moral dilemma when I realized my dad had decided not to buy me a car for my birthday. If this was some kind of moral test, I guess I flunked it because I wanted that car so much I tried blackmail. I bought a piece of junk for myself that was so embarrassingly awful that my dad would have to get me a new car, just so I would get rid of the wreck. It worked. I now drive a red Corvette.

Sometimes I tell myself that Dad really wanted to give me a sports car anyway and that I just made it easy for him. Sometimes I tell myself that I'm a decent, hard-working kind of guy and I deserve a great car. But other times when my father starts shaking the newspaper and yelling that nobody has any moral backbone anymore, I feel that I'm a prime example of what he's talking about. And the worst part is—I don't even regret it.

Ann Lee Smith

Last week, when I got back my history test, I was pleased to see that I had a hundred. When the questions were reviewed in class, however, I discovered that I had actually missed two questions that Mrs. Hicks had failed to mark wrong. My moral dilemma was whether or not to call the error to her attention.

I did point out the error, and immediately I felt much better. I would rather have a B that I earned honestly than an A that I had gotten dishonestly.

"You're kidding!" said Michael.

Ann Lee blushed. "Michael, why are you reading over my shoulder?"

"Michael," said Mrs. Armstrong. "What are you doing?"

"Just sharpening my pencil, Mrs. Armstrong." He held the pencil up.

"Well, sharpen it, then, and get back to your desk."

Jesse McCracken

My dilemma is that I love a girl whose family members are enemies of my family. It's not exactly a moral dilemma. I guess you would call it a conflict between love and family loyalty. It's such a mess, not just for me but for all the other people involved, that I don't see any solution. There probably isn't any solution. It's driving me crazy.

I wish I loved Terri Hartley. My life would be pretty simple then.

Jesse covered his paper with his hand. His gray eyes were cold as he looked up at Michael. "Read my stuff, Dessaseaux, and I'll break your kneecaps."

"Hey, no problem, Jesse. I was just, uh, stooping

down to get my pencil. See? Wouldn't dream of reading your stuff.''

"Michael, when are you going to get back to your desk?"

"Any minute, Mrs. Armstrong. See? I'm on my way."

Michael sat down at his desk and began to write.

Michael Dessaseaux

My moral dilemma concerns a conflict between the individual's right to privacy and the artist's need to know the workings of the human heart. I do not find this very tricky. Art, you might say, lives above moral considerations. And in the artist's view, to observe is neither right nor wrong, it is only essential. There are, however, certain practical considerations which may impede an artist in his search for truth—a shortage of pencils, for example, or the tendency of violence exhibited by certain philistines who shall be nameless.

Susan Brantley

Dear Mrs. Armstrong, I know we are supposed to be writing about a moral dilemma, but this other problem is bugging me to an extent that I just can't think straight. I mean, night and day I think of nothing else but this problem—if you can call it a problem. I mean, it's thrilling! It's intriguing! It's *life!*

Someone is putting love letters in my locker! I keep trying to tell myself it is probably somebody unspeakably dorky, but I can't make myself believe that. Just from reading the letters I can tell the writer is cool, strong, and passionately in love.

But who fits that description? Absolutely no one. I mean, to look at the vacant faces of the boys I know, you'd figure they didn't have a thought in the world beyond what's for lunch. I have to get behind that façade if I'm going to discover who has this thrilling passion for me.

For a while I thought that maybe it was Blake, but now I'm not so sure. Would a boy who is passionately in love recoil when you touched him? The answer is no. *Unless* he were deeply neurotic, that is, like the sort of guy who shows up in those case studies we read in psychology class. I intend to carefully explore the question of whether Blake is neurotic in the days ahead.

Nine

Susan surveyed the kids around the lunch table. "Did you know that psychologists can find out a lot about people just by asking them questions?"

"No kidding. Give us an example." Ann Lee's helpful response was no accident. She had been carefully coached by Susan.

"Like these questions on standardized psych tests." Susan produced an index card and read from it. " 'I enjoy parties. Generally. Usually. Seldom.' "

"We all know you like parties, Susan," said Michael.

She turned to Blake. "What about you, Blake?"

He shrugged. "Depends on the party."

"Yeah, that kind of question is stupid," said Michael. "I don't see what it proves."

Susan frowned. He had a point. "Well, listen to this one, though. 'People often talk about me behind my back.' " She looked at them hopefully.

"You've got to get used to it," said Michael. "This

is that kind of school, and, hey, when you're a fascinating guy, what do you expect?''

"What about you, Blake? Do you think people often talk about you behind your back?"

He laughed. "I hope not."

She bit her lip. "Okay, listen to this one. 'My hands and feet are usually warm enough.' ''

Blake laughed.

"Pull yourself together, Susan." Michael punched her arm. "Man, these are not the questions that touch the human heart. You are totally on the wrong track, take it from me."

"I think it's interesting," said Rainey.

Susan shot her a grateful look.

"I think so, too," said Ann Lee. "You might find out things about yourself and others you didn't even suspect. I understand the things they can do with these psychological tests are amazing."

"Give me a break," said Michael. "The things you really want to know about people, they don't even touch. Like 'Are you going to pay me back if I lend you five dollars?' Now, there's a question for you. Rick Snyder still owes me five dollars from last April. Or, I know a good question. How about 'Do you think I'm good-looking?' ''

"No," said Blake. "I don't. But then I prefer girls."

The boys snickered.

"Has anybody noticed how hard it is to have a serious conversation around here?" asked Susan.

"Why would anybody want to have a serious conversation?" Michael asked. The two boys grinned at each other.

"What are some other questions on the test?" asked Rainey.

"This is ridiculous," said Michael. "If I wanted to take a test I'd be in class. Forget these stupid questions. Want to see a neat trick?" He flipped an olive into the air and caught it in his mouth. "That one's easy," he said. "But watch this."

He was holding an olive between his curled lip and his nose when he became aware that the table was unusually quiet. He turned and found himself staring at the waist of Mr. Bennett's three-piece suit. The olive fell into his lap and rolled to the floor.

"Playing with food, I see," said Mr. Bennett. "So we meet again, Dessaseaux. I want to see you in detention tomorrow morning, seven-thirty sharp." The principal pivoted smartly and marched out the door.

Rainey watched him leave. "I'd like to give our principal a psychological test."

"I know what you mean," said Blake. "It's funny the way he patrols all the time—the lunch room, the parking lot. I thought nobody liked doing that. The teachers are always sneaking off when they have bus duty or cafeteria duty. What's with him?"

"Yeah, what ever happened to principals overseeing the broader educational issues," said Michael bitterly.

"We live in a police state," said Susan. "It's just like that book *1984*." She stood up. "Excuse me while I stuff my regimented milk carton into the regimented trash."

Ann Lee followed Susan out of the cafeteria. "Could you tell anything from your questions?"

Susan shrugged. "Inconclusive. You heard it, Ann Lee."

"Maybe you should be more direct. Maybe you should just say, 'Blake, have you been writing me love letters?' "

Susan looked at her aghast. "You must be out of your mind, Ann Lee. I can't ask him that. If it wasn't him and it got around, people would be laughing at me all over school."

"Just an idea."

Michael had an appointment with the school counselor after school that day. Mrs. Cahoon was not the person he would have chosen to confide in. She was an elderly woman with bony shoulders and faintly pursed lips, which looked as if they were perpetually on the verge of saying no. Also she fidgeted constantly with paper clips. But when he realized that she was actually being paid to sit there and listen to him talk about himself, he could feel himself growing expansive. He leaned back in his chair. "You know, by the time I was in the third grade, I knew I wasn't like the other kids."

Mrs. Cahoon looked suddenly alert. "In what way, Michael?"

"For one thing, I was a lot bigger. Heck, by the time I was twelve I weighed one hundred sixty. I had to be careful not to step on the other kids' little bitty feet. But more important, there was this—how can I say it—this sensitivity, this interest in film, in the world of the imagination. Now back when I was in the fourth grade—"

"Perhaps we can just stick to the present for a while. Your request for an appointment was marked 'Emergency.' Could you explain that to me?"

Michael glanced at the closed door behind him. 'Uh, anything I say in here will be totally confidential, won't it?"

"Within reason."

"I need a straight answer on this, Mrs. Cahoon."

"I only mean that some things are so serious I can't promise confidentiality. If you were a danger to yourself or others, for example."

"It's not that bad. To tell you the truth, I just happened to bump Mr. Bennett with my bike and he got bent out of shape. Not literally bent, you understand. I barely touched him." Michael shifted uneasily in his seat. "So I told him I had a lot of personal problems I wasn't at liberty to disclose, and that was why I wasn't exactly concentrating on my driving."

"I see. Well, why don't we talk about these personal problems of yours for a minute."

"All right." Michael smiled and settled himself comfortably. "For one thing, I did this stupid thing a couple of years ago. I started smoking. You know in old movies, they're always smoking. The sexy, no-good woman blows smoke in the detective's face and the detective always has a cigarette dangling from his lower lip. I guess the prop people glue it there. His room's so thick with smoke it looks like they're burning a tire off camera. It looked kind of cool to me, you know? Decadent. But what I didn't realize is it stands to reason that a guy who can't eat just one Frito should never pick up a cigarette. Now that I've started, I just can't kick it. And the thing is, you may not have noticed this, but times have changed since they made those old movies. Nowadays when you light a cigarette, people act like you're a leper. They say you're smelling up their car or they make you go outside on the back porch and stand between the hanging baskets when you light up. Their parents stare at you and say you're a bad influence. I mean, take it from me, it's bad. I've tried everything to stop."

Mrs. Cahoon frowned. "I can see that's a problem,

but it's not exactly distracting you from what you're doing, is it?''

"Oh, I don't know. Sometimes I get these gross nicotine fits.''

"Let me put this another way, Michael. What exactly were you thinking when you hit Mr. Bennett with your motorcycle?''

"Not to say actually hit him. Grazed him, actually. Barely touched him.''

"Well, then.''

"Nothing.''

"You were thinking of nothing?''

"I have to concentrate on what I'm doing. The slowing down and stopping is a little bit tricky. The fact is, I'm still getting the hang of it. I haven't had the bike very long.''

"Are you telling me that you can't drive it?''

"I'm better now. That was a week ago that I hit Mr. Bennett. I've gotten a lot more practice.''

Mrs. Cahoon tore up the yellow slip with Michael's name on it and dropped it in the wastebasket. Michael watched her uneasily.

"Michael, why don't you just give Mr. Bennett a wide berth the next time you're coming in for a landing and I'll report to him that you seem to be doing much better.''

"You mean, I don't have to come see you anymore?''

"I'm a busy woman. Just try to stay out of trouble.''

"You mean, you don't want to hear all about my early life?''

She pursed her lips. "No.''

"Okay. Well, I'll be seeing you.''

He walked out to the parking lot, whistling, and got on his bike. He slipped his helmet over his head and zipped up his bomber jacket. The bike roared, vibrating under him with a vigor that shook his teeth. He tore out of the parking lot. The autumn sky was ominously dark and a fresh wind tumbled a piece of crumpled paper down the street in front of him. He turned onto Sunset Avenue. Hoping to beat the rain, he speeded up as he headed directly east toward home.

Suddenly raindrops spattered on his visor and the traffic light ahead of him blurred into splashes of scarlet. Soon rain began coming down in earnest, drumming against his helmet. It was streaming off his jacket and dark patches showed where the leather was getting soaked. Water dribbled stickily down his collar, and his legs itched where his wet pants legs flapped against bare skin.

Abruptly he made the decision to take a shortcut at the sign that marked U.S. 301. He sped down the ramp toward the highway. Rain was coming down in sheets now, and Michael could barely make out the road ahead. When he came off the ramp, a truck shot out from the underpass bearing straight at him. Instinctively, he veered out of its path. His front wheel hit the dirt and the bike spun and pitched him over the handlebars into the mud. A searing pain bit into him and for a second he was stunned and breathless. He could taste the faint saltiness of blood in his mouth where he had bitten his tongue. Less than two yards away, the big trucks whistled as they swept by, spewing wind and water. His bike was half on the clay shoulder and half on the paved road. He knew the truckers could see it because they were swerving to avoid it. His fingers dug into the mud and he tried painfully to push himself up. He felt a sharp pain and then a black curtain seemed to come down before his eyes.

When Michael came to, he knew he had been unconscious for a while because he was in a puddle of water that had not been there before. On the highway nearby, water hissed and whistled under the wheels of speeding cars. He wondered how many hundreds of cars and trucks had passed by his inert body. He straightened his uninjured leg very gingerly. It was obvious something was wrong with his left foot because it hurt unbelievably when he tried to move. The rest of him wasn't in the greatest shape either.

Through the haze of rain, he saw the lights of a filling station ahead. If he could only get that far, he'd be okay. Unless he was run down, that is. A figure in denim and brown leather was not very visible in a rainstorm. He would have to be careful to stay well clear of the highway. He gritted his teeth and carefully propped himself up on an elbow.

A Mazda, its lights blazing in the rain, sheered off to miss the motorcycle, then slowed and pulled off the road. The driver's door opened and a yellow-clad figure got out.

"Are you okay?" a girl's voice called.

"Sure, I do this just for kicks," yelled Michael. He regretted the words as they came out of his mouth. This was no time to be smarting off. "I think I may have broken something," he added more humbly.

His rescuer, sensibly dressed in boots and a voluminous slicker, knelt beside him. He thought her pale oval face with its haunting dark eyes was the most beautiful thing he had ever seen. "I think I'd better call an ambulance," she said. "You don't seem to be in shock, but I don't think I'd better try to get you in my car in case there are internal injuries. You're breathing okay, aren't you? No dizziness or nausea, anything?" A shower of spray hit them as a truck roared by. "I think we'd better get you a little farther off the road. Do you think you can roll over?"

A groan escaped Michael. He felt very strange. He wondered if his ribs were broken and were even now puncturing his lungs or something awful like that. Awkwardly, he managed to roll to the patch of weeds that grew on the edge of the muddy clay shoulder.

"You should be okay here. I'm going to call an ambulance. It may seem like it takes a long time but don't worry, I'll be back."

"You'll always find me at home." Michael winced. "Jeeves will show you in."

The girl smiled at him. When she got back to her car she waved reassuringly back at him, then got in and drove off.

It seemed an eternity that he lay in the mud with the rain drumming on his helmet, thinking about death and permanent disability. Finally the flashing red lights of an ambulance appeared. Michael was hoisted onto a stretcher and shoved in the back of the ambulance. The girl in the yellow slicker climbed in after him and peeled off her dripping raincoat. Michael saw that she was wearing a white uniform and a plastic I.D. tag with her picture on it.

"I was on my way to work when I spotted you," she said.

He winced. "Lucky for me."

"Hang on. You're going to be all right."

X-rays revealed that Michael had a sprained ankle, a couple of cracked ribs, and multiple contusions. He had also broken a small bone in the arch of his left foot.

He was obviously going to be out of school for a while, so Blake brought him his school assignments at home that evening.

"I've got to stay in bed till the swelling goes down, maybe a couple more days," Michael explained. "Then I'll get a walking cast and I'll be fine." He winced. "Except when I laugh."

"Then I guess you'll be back for the trig test on Friday."

"I don't know. Thinking about trig, all of a sudden I feel very, very weak."

"Don't worry. Mr. Amerson said you won't have to take it till Tuesday."

"On Tuesday I may have a relapse." Michael shifted his position gingerly and groaned. "Jeez, and I didn't even get her name."

"What?"

"The nurse. The one who rescued me. And she was wearing a name tag even." He hit his head with his hand. "Ouch. I shouldn't have done that. Even as we speak I am slowly turning purple and green all over. I'll be a giant walking bruise. But I've got to find that girl. It shouldn't be hard. She works at the hospital. All I have to do is hang around at the hospital cafeteria until I see her. But what if she brings her lunch? No, I can work that out. If it's no go with the cafeteria, then I'll hang around outside. I'll find out when the shifts change and park by the entrance and watch for her. No wait, I've got it. I'll comb all the reserved parking spaces until I find a Mazda and then I'll just camp by the car until she comes. Yeah, that's it."

"You didn't get a concussion or anything, did you? You're sounding kinda weird."

Michael fell back onto his pillow. "No, I didn't get a concussion, idiot. Jeez, I wish you could have seen her—those eyes of hers, those dimples. I mean this is *the* woman. I've got to see her again."

"But if she's a nurse she must be twenty-one, twenty-two. Even older."

"What difference does that make? I'm no age snob."

"Yeah, but she's not going to want to go out with some high-school kid."

"Blake, ole buddy, you've got to quit thinking about yourself as a high-school kid and start thinking of yourself as a human being. That's what I do. Say, do you think if I got myself put in a hypnotic trance I might be able to remember what was on the name tag? I've read about things like that."

"You're already in a trance, man."

"There was something about her—I tell you, I was blown away. I can't believe I was such a numbskull as to let her get away without finding out her name."

Blake got up. "If you need anything else, just give me a call. Don't worry about trig. I'll explain to Mr. Amerson that you're delirious."

TEN

t least he can't ride his motorcycle until he's healed," said Susan. "That's something. That means he can't do anything much to kill himself for the next six weeks."

Blake shook his head. "I don't know. He says he's getting a walking cast in a few days and pretty soon he'll be getting around fine."

"I just realized," said Susan, "that he might still be in the cast when it's time for the dance."

"If there is a dance," put in Ann Lee.

"You mean you haven't talked to Mr. Bennett yet? I thought you would have done it by now," said Susan.

"You know I haven't. I asked the kids at student council, but nobody would go with me. They're all in favor of it, but they're all afraid. They think he'll yell at us." She shivered a little. "They may be right."

"Nothing ventured, nothing gained," said Rainey. "I'll go with you."

"Well, gee, thanks, Rainey. I didn't know you were interested in the dance."

"I'll go, too," said Susan.

Ann Lee took a deep breath. "All right then, I guess I'll make an appointment. I mean, there's no reason to put it off any more. I've already talked to everybody else and got everything lined up. I'm ready to make a strong argument. I think when I show him how carefully I've planned this, we might be able to persuade him." She made an effort to look optimistic.

Ann Lee arranged an appointment with Mr. Bennett for just after school on Tuesday. That gave her a day to dread it, and by Tuesday at three she had practically turned to jelly.

"We have an appointment with Mr. Bennett," she told the school secretary in a faint voice.

"He's expecting you. You can go right in."

Ann Lee's mouth felt so dry she was afraid she might not be able to speak when she actually faced him. She wondered what crazy instinct for self-destruction had given her the idea of trying to organize a school dance.

"Ah." Mr. Bennett's eyes narrowed as the girls entered his office. "A delegation. I understand you want to talk about—a dance."

"Y-yes, sir," said Ann Lee. At first she couldn't think of what she had planned to say. She seemed to have frozen.

Rainey looked at her. "Ann Lee is going to outline the plans she's made for the dance."

"Uh, yes, sir, we feel that with careful planning, we can have a safe and orderly dance." She was sure her eyes were glazed, but at least she was talking. "Mrs. Ebb, Mrs. Sheridan, and Mr. Weeks have already agreed

WILD TIMES AT WEST MOUNT HIGH

to be chaperones. Mrs. Torres says the home ec classes will make the refreshments, and Mike Deever's dad, who is a police officer, says he will check student I.D.s at the door. We're going to have the punch bowl attended at all times to ensure that it won't be spiked.'' She took a deep shuddering breath. ''I would like to point out that hundreds of schools have dances every year with no disorderly incidents. I think we deserve a chance to show that we can do that, too, sir.'' Her knees were close to buckling, and Mr. Bennett's expression had not changed.

Seeing that Ann Lee had run dry, Rainey picked up the ball and improvised quickly. ''The student council supports this dance one hundred percent,'' she said. ''Social events promote school unity and healthy school spirit.''

Mr. Bennett pressed the tips of his fingers together. He looked at the three girls in silence until Ann Lee could feel sweat gather and run down her back. None of the girls could think of anything else to say.

Finally he spoke. ''Very well. I am a reasonable man.'' He gave them a thin smile. ''I am willing to give the students a chance to show that they can behave like mature young adults instead of hooligans at a school function. But—if there are any problems, any problems at all, we won't be having any more dances. Period.''

Ann Lee would have liked to know what exactly fell under the category of ''problems,'' but she felt that to have asked for clarification would have ended the meeting on the wrong note.

The girls looked at one another and hurriedly fled the principal's office.

''That man is very strange,'' said Rainey when they

got outside. "Did you notice how he enjoyed watching us squirm?"

"We weren't much help to you, Ann Lee," Susan said apologetically. "I couldn't think of anything to say. The fact is, I was too scared to speak. It was like my tongue was stuck to the roof of my mouth. It's something about the way he looks at you with those beady eyes."

"You were lots of help. You gave me moral support."

Susan grabbed Ann Lee's arm. "But the big thing is, we did it. Can you believe it! He actually said yes!"

"I just hope nothing goes wrong. You heard him. If there are any problems, no more dances."

"How can there be any problems?" asked Susan. "The place will be crawling with parents and teachers. Frankly, I think you may have even overdone it on the number of parents and teachers. It sounded like you've lined up as many chaperones as kids."

"I thought it was better to err on the side of caution. And don't say anything. I know what you're thinking. You're thinking I always err on the side of caution. But just remember that without me, there wouldn't be any dance at all."

"You get all the credit," said Susan.

"Or the blame." Ann Lee looked suddenly gloomy.

"You worry too much," Rainey said. "Even if it's a mess, we can't be any worse off than we are now."

"You're right. This is a victory. I should enjoy it. But we've got a lot of work to do. An awful lot of work. Don't forget, Susan, you said you'd be the head of the decoration committee."

"I'll help out, too," said Rainey.

"Oh, good," Ann Lee said absently. "I've got to call my mother now. I didn't know when to tell her to pick me up because I wasn't sure how long this was going to take us."

"Don't bother. I'll give you a ride home," said Susan. There was the briefest of pauses. "Do you need a ride home, Rainey?"

"No thanks. I've got my car."

"Oh, right. I forgot." Susan nudged Ann Lee. "Come on, I want to go by my locker first. See you later, Rainey." Susan and Ann Lee trotted off in the direction of A wing.

Rainey watched them go. Their hurried confidences, their suppressed excitements had not gone by her. Once in chemistry class, she had seen Susan pass a letter in a cream-colored envelope to Ann Lee and had watched Ann Lee's face change color when she read it. That they didn't let her in on the secret didn't bother her. She had seen one of Jesse's letters—written on cream-colored paper—and she had a pretty good idea what they were whispering about without being told.

What bothered her was not their secret, but the way they seemed to forget she was around sometimes—those slight awkward pauses, the faint surprise when she spoke that showed they hadn't remembered she was there. She figured it was because she wasn't rich and lived in a different neighborhood from them, but she wasn't in the habit of brooding on what couldn't be helped. She squared her shoulders and reminded herself that being rich only sapped your initiative. Sucking in her cheeks, she thrust her hands in her pockets and walked to her car, whistling softly to herself.

Ann Lee and Susan ran to the locker alcove at the end of A wing. Susan flung her locker open at once but was greeted by nothing but books. She looked at Ann Lee with dismay. "Maybe I'm not going to get any more love letters."

"Maybe you said something to hurt his feelings, whoever he is."

"How can I hurt his feelings when I don't even know who he is?"

"Well, why else would he suddenly quit writing?"

Susan stiffened. "Wait a minute, Ann Lee. Maybe it's somebody who *couldn't* write. Maybe it's somebody who hasn't been in school lately. Like *Michael!*"

"Michael?"

"He was standing right here watching when I got the first letter. I thought it was kind of funny the way he kept shuffling those books. It was like he was looking for an excuse to hang around. He could have been watching to see my reaction when I read it."

"Michael?"

"You're repeating yourself. It's getting on my nerves, Ann Lee."

"I'm sorry, but I mean, we know Michael pretty well. Those letters just don't sound like him."

"They don't sound like anybody. We've been all over that. Love letters sound different from the way people talk. Okay, it doesn't look like his handwriting, but people can *disguise* their handwriting. Remember the time he kissed my hand? And I thought he was just clowning around, but maybe he was expressing his deepest feelings. When I think about it, there was a kind of reverent awe in his gesture, like the way knights of old acted with their lady loves."

"You don't think the letters might be—well, a joke?"

"I don't see anything funny about them. We always *thought* Michael was a joker, but that sort of pose can be a mask for deep, intense feelings. Michael is probably a very sensitive boy underneath.''

''I still say if it's Michael it has to be a joke.''

''You don't think Michael is capable of deep and tender feelings?''

''But what about your theory that it was Blake who wrote the letters? What about that?''

''I haven't given up on it. I'm keeping it in mind. I'm considering all the possibilities. It threw me off the way Blake sort of backed off from me, but I have to remember that he may be really, really repressed. I mean big-time repressed. We've been learning about that kind of thing in psychology class. Sometimes these repressed people don't even know *themselves* what they feel like.''

''That doesn't sound like Blake to me.''

''Think about how polite he is. That's a sort of repression, isn't it?''

''I guess.''

''I just hope whoever it is hasn't given up.'' Susan's eyes took on a faraway look. ''I mean, those letters are absolutely the most beautiful thing in my life!''

Over the next few days news of the upcoming dance spread quickly. People stopped Ann Lee in the hall and offered to help, and after creative writing class, Mrs. Armstrong congratulated her personally on her success in getting permission. Ann Lee was elated. At last she felt she was at the center of things. For once, people were actually paying more attention to her than to Susan.

Friday, Michael came back to school leaning on a crutch. ''I'm a wreck,'' he groaned at his locker. ''I'm a remnant of my former self.''

''This can't be all bad,'' Susan said lightly. She

sneaked a surreptitious glance at him, not sure whether to kid around or not. She wanted to be careful not to mock any deep, tender feelings he might be struggling to express.

"I should have known better than to expect sympathy from you, oh, heartless one," he said.

Susan looked at him expectantly, but he made no move to kiss her hand. Of course, she reminded herself, he *was* in pretty bad shape.

"Didn't they give you anything for the pain?" asked Ann Lee.

"Demerol. But I like to keep my head clear for trig. Don't worry about me, I told Mr. Amerson, I'll just bite on a bullet or something. No kidding, guys, just about every part of me hurts except my teeth."

"Does this mean you'll be selling your motorcycle?" inquired Ann Lee.

"Not a chance. I'm just getting the hang of it."

"Michael"—Susan regarded him anxiously—"you wouldn't expect a girl to ride on that thing. I mean, assuming you ever started going with somebody on a more or less serious basis, I mean."

"Listen to that! What is it about women? I swear, they can read your mind. How did you know that I was interested in somebody?"

Susan swallowed. "Wild guess."

"Any luck yet?" asked Blake.

"Good grief, this is my first day out of bed, man. Give me a chance."

"Who is it, Michael?" asked Rainey. "Who have you fallen for?"

Susan paled. Trust Rainey to come bluntly to the point.

"I'm not telling." Michael looked pointedly at Blake.

"*Some* people don't think I've got a chance. *Some* people think I'm out of my mind. Well, we'll see, that's all."

On the way to English class Susan and Ann Lee had a hurried consultation.

"What do you think?" Susan shifted her books to her hip.

"It is awfully funny that all of a sudden Michael is talking about falling for somebody," Ann Lee admitted. "I can't remember that he ever talked about any girl except Greta Garbo."

"I don't know. It just doesn't make sense." Susan frowned. "Michael doesn't act like he's got a thing for me."

"How is he supposed to act?"

"Oh, you know. They sort of look at you a lot and then if you look back at them they drop things."

"Oh."

"Michael's not like that."

"Michael's not an ordinary guy, though."

"That's for sure."

Because Michael was limping along with the help of a crutch, Blake had to carry his books to chemistry. "How long are you going to be on that thing?" Blake asked.

"Not much longer, I hope. It really slows me down and I've got to be sharp for the pursuit."

"You aren't thinking about bringing the nurse to the dance, are you?"

"Blake, a woman like that is not interested in a high-school dance."

"I'm thinking of asking Susan to it."

"Susan? Why Susan?"

"Because I know she'll say yes."

"Blake, Blake, any girl would say yes. Your looks, your Corvette. Think about it."

"Yeah, well, we don't all have your self-confidence."

"Not that anything's wrong with Susan. Susan's okay."

Blake shrugged.

"Man, the strength of your feeling just bowls me over. Haven't you ever wanted something, I mean really really wanted something?"

Blake smiled self-consciously. "The Vette."

"Sheesh. A car. Sure, it's a great car, but—it *is* just a car." Michael waved a hand dismissively. "Well, have fun at the dance."

"So you just aren't going?"

"Not me." Michael smiled at him wolfishly. "I'll be busy staking out the hospital parking lot."

ELEVEN

*T*hat night Michael showed up at Blake's house in a state of high excitement. "I found her. There she was in the cafeteria! Blake, no kidding, she is even better than I remembered. I mean, she's great! I know you're thinking this is just something physical, but that's not it. Well, sure, that's part of it, but the big thing is she's just such a beautiful person. You know what I mean?"

Blake closed the door to his room. He wasn't sure he wanted his mother to hear this.

"So, did you say anything to her?"

"I didn't have to. She recognized me. She came over and asked how I was getting along, inquired after my health, man." Michael closed his eyes tight. "We were so close— I mean, there we were breathing the same air molecules, sitting at the same little table. Our knees were practically touching. She has this cute little mole just at the end of her eyebrow. Did I mention her dimples?"

"You mean she sat down and ate with you?"

97

"Yeah, it was great. You know, it turns out she's interested in old movies, too? How about that? She actually comes from New Jersey, but she went to college down here so when she got a job offer from West Mount General, she figured why go back up there and battle all that ice and snow. Her mother's dead and her dad's remarried and has a couple of young kids, disgusting, really. He must be forty or fifty. I think she's lonely."

"Are you trying to tell me she said she'd go out with you?"

"That's right. I'm going to take her to Hunan Station. She likes Chinese food."

"Does she have any idea how old you are?"

"Actually, I sort of gave the impression that I was taking off some time from school to get my head together, working at menial jobs and all."

"You told her you were a high-school dropout?"

"You know your voice starts to squeak when you get all worked up. You have to watch that. That kind of thing really turns women off. Naturally, I didn't tell her I was a high-school dropout, dope. I acted like I was taking a year out from college."

"How can you lie like that?"

"It's not lying exactly. I mean, what are a few years here or there?" Michael leaned back on the bed and smiled happily.

Monday, another letter was in Susan's locker.

Susan, I don't know how long I can go on like this. I've tried to get over it but I can't. When I see you smiling at some other guy, I feel as if little bits and pieces of me are dying. I want more than anything to find out if you feel at all the way I do. I think about you, I dream about you. I want to touch you. Every day we're close, yet there's an invisible wall keeping us apart.

Clutching the letter in her hand, Susan edged her way past a couple of giggling girls and some tall guys in sweatshirts. Ann Lee was pulling books out of her locker. Susan thrust the letter under her nose. "So close," she whispered. "Look at it. It's got to be Blake. The invisible wall must be his shyness about telling me his feelings."

Ann Lee examined the letter carefully. "What made you decide it couldn't be Michael?"

"Ann Lee, I cannot believe that a boy who picks up an olive with his nose wrote those letters."

"I see what you mean."

"It's self-evident. I don't know why I didn't realize that before."

"Excuse me," said a boy in a letter sweater. "But could I get to my locker?"

The girls moved aside. Locker doors were banging all around them as people got their books for class.

"But there are hundreds of boys around here and you said yourself that you know a lot of them, so I don't see how you can be sure it's Blake."

"Well, whoever it is, I should know for sure pretty soon. He's got to make his move any minute. He practically says he is."

"Susan?"

Susan jumped. Blake had tapped her on the shoulder. She glanced quickly at his face, but she saw no sign that he had noticed the letter in her hand. She could feel the blood draining from her face. Now that she suspected the passion hidden behind that face, she felt almost afraid of him. She had known him all her life, but now she realized she didn't really know him at all.

"Uh, could I talk to you for a minute?" Blake tugged nervously at his nose.

Susan cast a panic-stricken glance at Ann Lee.

"I was just leaving." Ann Lee scooted out of the locker alcove without a backward glance.

Other kids were milling around banging books and kicking lockers closed. It was not exactly the ideal setting for romantic confidences.

"I was just wondering," Blake said, "if you'd like to go to the dance with me."

Susan looked at him with wide eyes. This was it. This was The Move!

"Of course, if you think I'm asking too far ahead of time or something—" he went on.

"No, n-no," she stuttered. "That's fine. I mean, that's great. I'd love to go with you. I think it's going to be really special, don't you? I mean"— she looked at him anxiously—"sort of romantic."

He shrugged.

Lines from the love letters echoed in Susan's head. "You are the melody in my heart, all day and all night my heart sings Susan." What could she do to make Blake feel secure enough to whisper those things in her ear? What could she do to make him understand that he didn't have to pretend indifference with her? "I like to dance," she said softly.

He flashed a sudden smile. "Me, too," he said. "Well, see you."

Susan stood for a moment, looking at Blake's retreating figure, feeling stunned by his smile. In the past when she'd been out with him it had just been like going out with one of the guys. But that was before she understood the depth of feeling behind his pleasant, easygoing façade. She had had no idea that he was such a complex person. But why should that surprise her? She was the same. Maybe everyone was. She went through the day caught up in meaningless superficialities, chatter and class assignments, while deep inside she was filled with fears, yearnings, and green, hopeful thoughts she didn't share with anyone. She had the feeling she was on the verge of a new and mature intimacy, a relationship in which she could share her deepest feelings. How strange to think that it was Blake, all the time, who had seen past her superficial silliness to the person inside!

Of course, she would have to be careful. He had made it abundantly clear that he was shy about his feelings. His first tender gropings toward openness must be carefully nurtured. She had to let him know that she would never laugh at him, that she understood and appreciated the way he felt.

Clutching her books close to her chest, she cautiously edged her way through the kids crowded into the locker alcove. A blow caught her right between the shoulders and she staggered. Her books fell thudding to her feet.

"Sorry," said a hoarse voice.

Susan looked around and was surprised to see Jesse. Suddenly her face felt as if it were drenched in hot water. He was the last person she had expected.

Someone hurrying past planted a foot squarely on Susan's creative writing notebook, squashing the metal spirals. Susan stooped down to rescue her books. Jesse bent over to help her. Her papers were scattered all over the grimy floor.

"Is this yours?" he asked. Looking straight in her eyes, he handed her the love letter.

Susan gulped and swiftly stuck it inside a book. She didn't think she could stand it if Jesse laughed at her. Once she thought she cared about him. And even when it turned out that he was a different human being entirely from what she thought, her pulse still did odd things when she was around him. It was so strange to have him hating her, strange to have that eerie distance between them.

"Thank you." Susan blindly took the papers from him and hurried away. When she glanced over her shoulder, she was shaken to see that Jesse was still watching her with that oddly intent look. She wondered if he had hit her on purpose. Was it possible that he was actually dangerous? She wouldn't have thought so, but then she never would have dreamed his father would shoot Muffin, either. It was a strange world. You heard of such awful things—terrorist attacks in Lebanon, gun feuds in the Ozarks, survivalist freaks living in the national forests. Who could say that bizarre things couldn't happen right at West Mount High? Muffin's death had ended Susan's calm certainty about the safety of her world, and as she made her way to class she felt chilly.

TWELVE

The following weekend, Blake's parents were away at a medical convention. He wasn't in the mood to pop something frozen in the microwave, so he went to a fast-food place for supper.

To his surprise, Rainey was standing behind the counter looking strangely domesticated in a grape-colored polyester uniform. He almost hadn't recognized her.

"I get paid today," she said. She punched his order into the keyboard. "As soon as I get off work at seven, I can bring you the next car payment."

"Don't worry about it. You can give it to me at school."

A blast of cool air swept into the restaurant, and Blake glanced over his shoulder.

"Hi, Rainey, Blake." Michael flung out his arms in greeting.

"Hi, Michael." Rainey smiled at him. "Want to order?"

"No thanks. Actually, I'm on kind of a health food kick."

Once Blake got his order, Michael followed him to a table, looking pleased with himself.

"Okay, out with it." Blake sat down and snapped open the Styrofoam box containing his fish nuggets. "How'd your date with the nurse go?"

Michael regarded the fried fish with the expression of a preacher considering sin. "That junk is full of saturated fat, you know."

"Sure, well, I'll worry about that later, okay? So what about the nurse?"

"Blake, old boy, this is the real thing. I'm serious. Our fortune cookies had identical fortunes. What do you think about that?"

"Quality control in the Chinese cookie factory ain't what it used to be."

" 'You will embark on an interesting adventure.' That's what they said."

"Fascinating."

"Look, do you want to hear about this or not?"

"I'm sorry. Sure, I want to hear. Go ahead." Blake realized he was a little down ever since he had asked Susan to the dance. Maybe asking her had been a mistake.

"It was funny, you know? We felt comfortable together right off. I realized that those giggling little girls at school are not for me. Cynthia—beautiful name, isn't it? Like the sound of a summer breeze—Cyn-thia. You wouldn't believe what that woman has to go through at the hospital—the responsibility she has! She's dealing with life-threatening illnesses on a daily basis and no support staff worth talking about."

"Hospitals have had to do a lot of cost cutting," Blake pointed out.

"And the doctors around here treat the nurses like servants. They don't give them the respect they should have as professionals. No wonder hospitals have trouble keeping people. Did you know they're having to import nurses from Ireland?"

"Yeah, yeah, but get to the point. What about you and her? Did that subject ever come up?"

"Well, hearing all that stuff about the doctors just made my blood boil. You know, all those guys want is somebody to bow and scrape to them. Half of them don't know what they're doing. One of them was even giving a patient the wrong dosage until Cynthia pointed it out. And he had the nerve to get all snippy with her about it."

"There are rotten apples everywhere."

"Oh, yeah, I forgot your father's a doctor. You've got a little bias there, Blake old boy. But the thing I'm getting at is that I want her to know that I respect her as a person. I don't want her to think I'm just using her, like those lowlifes at the hospital. I don't want to rush her. She's in a high-stress job and she doesn't have anybody she can unload to. She's got friends in Raleigh but she doesn't get away to see them that often. She needs somebody that she can talk to."

"This is sort of a platonic thing? Is that what you're telling me?"

"Well, not on my part, naturally. But I don't want to push her. I get such a charge out of just being around her. She's a sweet, old-fashioned sort of girl. We talked about how important it is to really give a lot of time to your children. Cynthia's crazy about children, and you know, when I'm talking to her I start getting this feeling that I'm crazy about children, too. It's funny because generally speaking the little brats get on my nerves. But when I'm with her I get this feeling that I just love them, that I'd want to have dozens of them.''

''I can't believe this. Are you telling me you're giving her all these signals that you're ready to settle down? Doesn't she have any *idea* that you're just a junior in high school?''

Michael glanced at his reflection in the big window. ''I look pretty mature for my age,'' he said complacently.

''You may *look* like you're ready for Medicare, but that doesn't change the fact that you're actually sixteen.''

''Blake, Blake, you worry too much. Cynthia thinks a couple ought to be married at least five or six years before they begin a family.''

''Oh, well, that changes everything.''

''You know while we were at that restaurant, though, the weirdest thing happened. I see this guy sort of slinking out of the booth in the corner and there's something kind of familiar about him, you know, so I turn around and check him out while he's at the cash register and, get this—it's Mr. Bennett.''

''He likes Chinese food. This is big news?''

''But that's not all. It looked to me like Bambi Whitney was with him.''

''Bambi Whitney, the senior? Bambi Whitney who danced on the table at Brian Chambless's end-of-the-year party?''

''The same. I can't be absolutely sure they were together because she didn't stick around. She went right on outside.''

"Even if she was, there's probably some perfectly ordinary explanation."

"Sure, like she was selling him Girl Scout cookies."

"Or band fruit."

"Or he could be counseling her."

"Right."

"But there was the slinking. You can't get away from that."

"Probably your imagination. Besides, when you think about it, even if he was there with Bambi, what's he doing that you aren't doing? He's older than she is, Cynthia's older than you are."

"I'm surprised at you, Blake. A man that age! It's disgusting. It's sick."

Blake shrugged.

"What's the matter with you? You don't seem exactly all here. Something on your mind?"

"Maybe." Blake hesitated. "Look, does it seem to you that Susan is awfully friendly to me lately?"

"Didn't you tell me you were going to ask her to the dance?"

"Yeah. I did."

"There it is, then. Girls get very weird about big dances."

"I've been out with Susan before, though. I took her to a couple of parties last year. Went to a ball game. She's never acted like this before."

Michael grinned. "The love of a good woman is a precious thing."

"Sure, sure, make fun of me. Do I make fun of you and your nurse?"

"All the time."

"Oh, come on. I don't."

"Look, Blake, your problem is easy to solve. If she's getting weird because you asked her to the dance, then un-invite her. Simple."

"I can't do that! Jeez, you and your crazy ideas."

"You're a slave to convention, that's all. No wonder you've got troubles. Well, I'd love to hold your hand some more about this, Blake old boy, but I've got to run. I'm meeting Cynthia at the hospital coffee shop."

Blake glanced down at the cast. "How are you getting around these days?"

"Borrowed my parents' car. It's got automatic transmission. No problem. My dad says I can drive it as much as I want. He even said he was glad to see I was starting to have a normal social life for a change, instead of sitting around watching the tube. He gave me an extra fifty dollars for expenses."

Blake covered his eyes with his hand. "Okay, good luck, my friend. You're going to need it, believe me."

Michael grinned. As he left he lifted both arms and expansively included all the diners in the restaurant in his boundless good will.

Blake reminded himself that Michael was riding for a fall. Still he envied that radiant grin. It must be nice to be so sure of yourself.

When Blake got home, he was surprised at how empty the house seemed. It looked forlorn, as if his parents had gone for good. The medical journals by his father's chair were in a neat stack, and the message blackboard in the kitchen had been washed clean. It gave him the creeps. Out the kitchen window he could see the lights on the top floor of Susan's house. He jerked on the window cord and let the blinds rattle closed. He didn't want to look at Susan's house.

He didn't feel that he understood girls, maybe because he didn't have any sisters. Asking Susan to the dance had seemed like a logical thing to do at the time. She liked to dance; he liked to dance. So far so good. And she was a good-looking girl, the type he'd be happy to be seen with. She seemed to flit from boy to boy, never into anything serious. Who could have guessed that asking her to a dance could make her all strange? For the past few days it seemed to him that she was always looking at him. She asked him questions. She listened very carefully to his answers. It was enough to drive a guy crazy.

He picked up the television schedule and checked it out—nothing on, as usual. Any other night he might have gotten Michael to come over, but Michael was tied up with his nurse. He rattled his keys in his pocket. Abruptly, he decided to go out.

When he went to the fast-food place where Rainey worked, he spotted the old car he had sold her. It must be time for her to be getting off pretty soon. Acting on an impulse, he turned his car into the parking lot.

A minute later Rainey came out the back door, her uniform over her arm. Blake stuck his head out the window. "Rainey! Over here!"

She came over to the car. "I haven't cashed my check yet, Blake. Sorry. I hadn't realized they wouldn't pay me in cash."

"Don't worry about it. You can give it to me later. Want to go for a ride? You could see the Vette do her stuff."

"Okay." She threw her uniform in the back seat and got in.

Blake was relieved to see that in her jeans and shirt she looked like herself once more. To put an exotic type like

109

Rainey into one of those polyester uniforms was a criminal waste of natural resources. There were already enough boring-looking people in the world. Rainey was definitely out of the ordinary. With her dark eyes and the way she held herself straight, she reminded him of the women he had seen in Arab countries walking down roads with pottery jars on their heads. His spirits began to lift a little.

Rainey stroked the Corvette's seat cushion. "You know, this is like stepping into a car advertisement, one of those where everything is shiny and new and the car is always on a open road or in the desert or something."

He pulled out onto Sunset. "I see what you mean. A car like this doesn't even seem to belong to real life. Like, sometimes I look at the homework piled on the seat and I sort of do a double-take, you know? It doesn't seem to belong there."

"Aren't you ever tempted to see how fast it will go? Just once?"

"Are you kidding? The last thing I want is to get busted. It'd be bye-bye Vette if that ever happened. My dad wouldn't think twice about yanking it, believe me."

Rainey had noticed before how kids with money worried about what their parents thought. It was as if they had extra-long childhoods.

Blake was frowning. "Rainey, you're a girl, aren't you?"

"Absolutely."

"Well, would you say that girls look on big dances as different from other dates? I mean, would you say they have more significance?"

"I guess. It's not like stopping off for pizza. You've got to get a special dress and stuff. It can run into money if you aren't careful."

"But you don't figure a girl thinks you're serious about her just because you ask her to a dance, do you?"

"I don't think so. Because lots of people just want to go to the dance. They might go to a dance with somebody they wouldn't normally even talk to. Like last year when Jennifer Mason went with that exchange student, Abdul. He didn't even speak much English, but he wanted to go to the dance, she wanted to go to the dance, so they went together. Sometimes people go to a big dance together even though they don't normally go out."

"That's kind of what I thought, too."

"Why are you asking? Is something bothering you?"

Blake hesitated. "Have you noticed anything funny about Susan lately?"

"Well, she hangs on every word you speak. Is that what you mean?"

"You've noticed it, too, then! It's not just my imagination. I tell you, it's driving me bonkers."

"It could be because of your car."

"What?"

"Your car is your identity—that's what Susan was going around saying after her psych class did that survey about cars. Remember?"

"Yeah, but—"

"Maybe she's getting all excited about riding in it. Maybe she wants to play this one dance into some kind of permanent arrangement so she can ride in a Corvette any time she wants."

"You really think so?"

Rainey shook her head regretfully. "Not really. I know Susan's not one of the world's great brains, but I can't believe she actually has gotten you mixed up with your car. How about this—maybe when you asked her to the dance the scales fell from her eyes and she realized you were the one for her.''

"Oh, come on. I don't believe that.''

They drove for a moment in silence. Rainey watched the streetlights go by outside and struggled with her conscience.

"There is one other possibility,'' she said hesitantly.

"Well, come on, out with it. I hope it's better than the ones you've come up with so far.''

Rainey avoided Blake's eyes. "Did you know that Susan has been getting anonymous love letters?''

"No joke! Did she tell you that?''

"Not exactly. But I, uh, had a clue that was what was going on, and subsequent investigation bore it out.''

Blake blanched. "Are you telling me that she thinks I'm the one who wrote them?''

"It's possible.''

Blake drove slowly down Sunset. He was breathing heavily. "But wait a minute. Why doesn't she ask me about them?''

"Maybe she thinks you're embarrassed. Maybe she thinks that's why you haven't signed your name.''

"We've got to set her straight! There's no telling what kind of goop is in them.''

Rainey cleared her throat. "Actually, I happen to know what kind of goop is in them. If I may quote, 'You are the melody in my heart. All day and all night my blood sings Susan, Susan.' ''

His eyes widened. "Now you're scaring me, Rainey. No joke.''

Rainey said nothing. She waited to let what she had said sink in.

"You know,'' Blake said finally, "I wouldn't be a bit

surprised if you've hit it.'' He ran a finger around his collar, as if the car suddenly seemed unbearably warm and close. ''What else could make her act like this? I mean, it's not as if Susan hasn't been out with a lot of guys, some of them driving pretty decent cars, too. She's not the type to go all bananas just because you ask her to a dance. I thought that myself.'' He stared sightlessly ahead. ''But love letters—that's something else. I've got to tell her it's all a big mistake. But, jeez, how am I going to do that if she doesn't bring it up first? If we were wrong, she'd think I'd gone out of my mind. You are sure about this, aren't you, Rainey? This isn't just some wild guess?''

''I actually held one of the letters in my hand.''

''It's just so weird. I've never heard of anybody writing love letters. I mean, these days when you can just pick up the phone, most people don't write letters at all. Wait a minute, though. How did you see one if Susan didn't show it to you?''

''I found it in your car. You know, after you sold it to me.''

He was taken aback. ''You didn't think that I—''

''Oh, no!'' she said hastily. ''Certainly not.''

''But then how—how did it get in my car?''

Rainey didn't want to be the one to say it.

After a minute Blake said, ''Jesse?''

''I think so.''

Blake shook his head. ''No, it's got to be some kind of mistake. Jesse would never write love letters to Susan. They don't even speak to each other. You heard about all that stuff with Susan's dog, didn't you?''

''Sure. But look at it this way, Blake. If it is Jesse, he would *never* admit it.''

"Oh, no, this is worse than I thought."

Rainey glanced at the speedometer. "The cops will be raking us in if you keep stepping on the gas that way."

"Sorry." He slowed down. "Look, this just isn't possible. This can't be happening to me. The way you're telling it, it's like some weird kind of catch-twenty-two situation. I can't deny it because Susan won't ever tell me that she's gotten the letters, and Susan won't ever tell me because she thinks I'm embarrassed. Jesse won't ever admit it because officially he's on the outs with Susan, and also he thinks she might slap his face if he made a move. I don't know, Rainey. It's so Byzantine, it can't be true."

"Byzantine?"

"Ridiculously complicated."

"I don't know. It seems to hold together."

"In a minute, I'll wake up and this will all be a bad dream. I mean, jeez, all I did was ask a girl to a dance. What did I do to deserve this? Hey, I know what—I should do just what Michael suggested and uninvite her. Okay, it would be unbelievably rude and if my mother ever found out she'd probably kill me. But this is a desperate situation, and it needs desperate measures. What do you think? As a girl, I mean. I uninvite her. Wouldn't she wash her hands of me then?"

"I don't know. People are very peculiar about washing their hands of people. Just when you think they should, they don't. I've noticed it over and over again."

"How could this be happening to me?" There was a note of panic in his voice.

"Oh, come on. It's not the end of the world. So Susan gets all goopy with you, so she thinks you're in love with her—what's the big deal?"

Blake gave her a blank look, which told her he failed to appreciate her moderate point of view.

"Maybe you better take me back to my car," Rainey said at last. "I guess I shouldn't have told you all this."

Blake turned the car around. "No, no, Rainey. I'm glad you told me about it. No kidding. I really do appreciate it. It gives me some idea of what I'm up against." From the look on Blake's face, a person might guess he was up against a firing squad. "You don't think there could be some mistake, though, do you?"

Rainey shrugged. "Figure it out yourself."

When Blake let Rainey out beside her car, he didn't even say goodbye.

THIRTEEN

_R_ainey stood and watched Blake's taillights wink out of sight. She felt restless and uncomfortable. Her car, which only weeks before had represented the pinnacle of her desires, suddenly looked worn out and ugly.

Why had she told Blake about the love letters? The last thing she needed was to alienate Jesse. And what she had told Blake could easily get back to Jesse. If Susan confronted him with the truth, what was more natural than that he demand to know where she got her information? After Jesse found out she had squealed, she couldn't expect him to diagnose funny sounds under the hood for her, free of charge. And she didn't look forward to facing him when he found out, either. She had the feeling that he might have a frightening temper.

She felt disgusted with herself. Her character must be weakening, she decided, or else she was getting soft in the head. She hadn't been able to resist telling Blake that she had information valuable to him—that was her trouble. Her intentions had been good—she meant to help him out, after all. But there had also been some shabby satisfaction at seeing him go cold with fear at the thought of Susan.

She counted out the money in her wallet. Eight dollars and eighty-two cents. Just enough for a pizza, luckily. She didn't want to go right back to the empty trailer and worry how long it was going to take for Jesse to find out what she'd done. She needed something to cheer her up.

When she got to the pizza place, the parking lot was almost full. It was a popular hangout on Saturday nights, and she felt a little funny going in alone.

"Rainey!"

Michael waved to her from the other side of the restaurant. Relieved to see a familiar face, Rainey waved back and went over to him.

"Want to split a small one with double cheese?" he asked.

"Sure."

The jukebox played a throbbing melody, while waitresses scurried from one overstuffed booth to another, dodging kids who were on their way to the salad bar.

"I'm glad I ran into you," Michael said. "I'm not all that hungry. I've already had dinner, but I'm not ready to go home yet. I'm still on some kind of high, I guess. You just get off work? I guess you weren't ready to go home either, huh?"

She smiled weakly and sat down. She hoped Michael wasn't going to notice how preoccupied she was.

The pizza arrived and Michael bit into a slice, wiping a string of mozzarella away with one hand. "Rainey? You're a girl, aren't you?" He leaned on his elbows and regarded her closely.

"Yes, indeed," she said wearily. This was obviously not her night to be appreciated for herself, and she had clearly been out of her mind to think that Michael would notice her mood. "What's the trouble?"

"Nothing's the trouble, actually. I mean, everything's great, man. I'm in love."

"Do I get to know who it is, yet?"

"Cynthia." He breathed the syllables of her name reverently.

"Do I know her?"

"She's a nurse at the hospital."

"Oh."

"You're taking it a lot calmer than Blake did. He practically flipped out. Well, what I'm wondering is, how do you know when a girl's feelings for you are strictly platonic and when they're not?"

"That's hard to say."

"What kind of answer is that?"

"These things aren't cut and dried, Michael. Like I know this boy that I really like. We're friendly, but you know if he were to start coming on to me I'm not sure how it would be. Would it work or not? I just don't know."

"Who is this guy?"

"It's not you, so calm down."

"I didn't think that for a minute. You may view this as simple curiosity with no redeeming social value whatsoever."

"Well, it's really not important. I just told you we're just friendly."

"I accept that. If you won't tell me, you won't."

"So tell me about Cynthia."

"It's this way. My instincts tell me that with Cynthia I should take it slow. What do you think?"

"Seems like a good idea."

"I just don't want to mess this up. I mean, the last thing I want is for her to think I'm just hitting on her. This could be serious. You're great to listen to all this, Rainey."

"Sure. Any time." She promised herself she would check her clothes over carefully when she got home to make sure there was no sign on the back saying, "Tell your troubles to this girl."

Michael went on for some time about how Cynthia was opening the world of classical music to him and how for her sake he was giving up smoking and exchanging Fritos for natural foods. But obviously, Rainey thought, he had no intention of giving up pizza. One thing about talking to Michael, though, it was restful. He was such an enthusiastic talker that all Rainey had to do was nod once in a while.

Meanwhile she was busy trying to calculate the odds that Blake would confront Susan and the odds that Susan would confront Jesse. The trouble was she really didn't know Susan well enough to get a handle on how she'd respond to the news that Jesse had written the letters.

When Michael's tale of true love at last began to run down and the pizza was almost gone, he spotted a friend coming in and, with a quick farewell to Rainey, cut out to greet the other friend.

Rainey wrapped the remaining slice of pizza in a napkin and decided that on the whole the talk with Michael had done her good. Hearing other people's troubles helped her to keep her own in perspective. She got up and made her way through the crowded restaurant. No sooner had she stepped outside than she spotted Jesse's old red Camaro and gave a guilty start. The car looked more maroon than red under the parking lot floodlights, but she knew it was Jesse's. His face was in shadow and she couldn't see him clearly, but she would have known him anywhere by the deliberate way he walked.

"How's it running?" he yelled. He came straight over to her, his fair hair taking on a greenish cast under the lights.

"It runs fine," she said and gulped.

Jesse lifted the hood of her car and regarded its innards with affection. "It's beautiful, isn't it. Clean? Heck, you could eat off this engine. I put in that alternator myself. Found the part in that junkyard west of town. I used to be out at the junkyard all the time, keeping my eye out for good parts."

"Well, so far, I haven't had any trouble," Rainey said nervously. "Not a bit of trouble." *Go away,* she was thinking. *Go a-way!* He was making her very jumpy.

Jesse snapped the hood closed and raised his head to admire the pale night sky over the parking lot lights. He was leaning on her car. He was, in fact, leaning against the only door that opened. She didn't see how she could leave unless he moved.

She took the keys out of her purse and jingled them, hoping he would take this delicate hint, but he didn't appear to notice. She appreciated his interest in her car, but sometimes his poking around gave her the feeling she just had the car on loan. And now that she had betrayed him, her situation felt particularly delicate.

"Rainey," he said. "If you wanted to know what was on a girl's mind and you couldn't ask the girl about it, what would be the best thing to do?"

"I guess," Rainey said reluctantly, "the usual thing

is to ask her friends. You say something like, 'Hey, does Susan ever talk about me?' "

His eyes opened wide in shock.

"Th-that's just a name picked at random," she stuttered. "You might just as well say Cynthia, or Daphne, or, uh, Esmerelda." Now she understood how the police got those confessions from criminals. The poor suckers were probably such nervous wrecks they confessed before they realized it.

He was looking at her funny. "Are you getting at something, Rainey?"

"No! I'm not getting at anything! Uh, could I just get past you here, Jesse?" She coughed. "I need to be getting on home."

"You must have been getting at something," he insisted. "Have you been hearing anything about me and Susan?"

She shook her head vigorously.

"Well, why did you say Susan?"

"I don't know. I eat lunch with this girl named Susan, and I guess that's why the name was on my mind."

"Yeah, I know you do. Susan Brantley."

"That's right, your table is right near ours, isn't it? And I guess you know Susan. Well, I mean, of course you know Susan."

"Some."

Rainey rattled her keys again, but without much hope. Jesse was not only not moving, he looked frozen to the spot. "Well, there must be some reason her name came to your mind." He licked his lips. "Does she ever talk about me?"

"I guess your name has come up once or twice. She mentioned that you had bumped into her by her locker,"

Rainey admitted. In fact, she distinctly remembered that Susan had shuddered when talking about it, but it hardly seemed tactful to go into that.

"Is that all?"

"She seemed to think maybe you had run into her because you were mad at her."

"Oh."

Jesse looked so bleak that Rainey scarcely knew what to say. Talk about your awkward situations.

"Well, I guess I'd better be going," she said.

He moved aside. "I'm not mad at her," he said. "If it comes up again, you can tell her that."

"Susan and I aren't really friends, you know. It's just the usual chit-chat at lunch."

"Yeah," he said. "It's just it looks like she's got the wrong idea. You might just let her know."

"Maybe you should talk to her yourself."

He gave a bitter laugh. "Yeah." He patted the old car gently before turning away. "See you," he said.

FOURTEEN

The next week Ann Lee sat on the bed and watched as Susan stepped into her dress. The top was black and strapless, the skirt was billowing white organza littered with black polka dots. Looking in the mirror, Susan danced a few steps, trying to get the effect of the skirt in motion. "Tonight should be the most exciting night of the year. I've got a strapless black dress, I'm going with a good-looking guy, and he's driving a brand-new Corvette. Why am I so miserable?"

You want miserable? thought Ann Lee. *Try being the girl who serves the punch.* But she didn't voice that thought. She could never have been friends with Susan if she had let envy and bitterness get to her.

Susan stared at the mirror. "Blake is acting so weird, I just can't figure it out. I've been as warm and accepting and encouraging as I can be. I've been practically twining like a morning glory around him, but the more I come on to him the more standoffish he is. What's the good of somebody being in love with you if this is all that happens?''

"Maybe you've got it all wrong. Maybe he isn't the one who wrote the letters."

"But *who?*" Susan opened her desk drawer and pulled out a much-thumbed letter. "Listen to this one. ''My lovely, lovely Susan, it's tough to be near you, to smell your hair, to see the light of laughter in your eyes, and yet to be like a stranger to you. I want to hold you close to me; I want to share your thoughts, I want your hand to be folded tight in mine. But when I reach out for you I grasp nothing but air. Empty air.' '' Susan looked up. "This one was in my locker Thursday."

"He sounds depressed," commented Ann Lee.

"The point is, he sounds *close*. I mean, you can't smell my Apple Blossom shampoo from fifty feet away. This narrows it down a lot. We've already ruled out Michael. Who else can it be but Blake?"

"I know what! Why don't you make a seating chart of who sits next to you in every one of your classes, and then test the distance we can smell the Apple Blossom shampoo. We can mark off the distance with a measuring stick and then—"

"Ann Lee, this is not Clue. This is my life! I'm sick of this silly game. I want to know who's writing these letters!"

"I don't see what you can do about it, though."

"I'll tell you what I can do about it. I can put a classified ad in the school paper. I've already written it. 'Lover, come out of the closet or buzz off. Susan.' ''

"That's certainly blunt and to the point."

"You better believe it. I'm tired of fooling around."

*   *   *

Storm clouds had gathered over the city. The lights had been turned on inside the fast-food restaurant where Rainey worked for an hour though it was technically still daylight. Rainey's customers fell into two categories—those who were carrying furled umbrellas, and those who were watching the sky anxiously. An elderly man in a raincoat ordered a package of cookies and a soft-serve ice cream. "We couldn't expect this good weather to last," he commented.

Rainey pushed his change across the counter. "I just wish it would rain and get it over with." She looked out the big windows facing Sunset Avenue and saw that the streetlights were already lit, turned on automatically by photoelectric cells when the sky grew dark. Traffic was thin. Most Saturday drivers had decided to stay home with the storm brewing.

The store manager came out to the register. "You get off pretty soon, don't you, Rainey?" She nodded. "You go on home. Maybe you'll beat the rain."

"Thanks, Sal."

"If it starts coming down, drive slow, you hear? Those wet roads are murder."

Rainey lost no time getting away. The air outside was heavy with moisture, and the sky seemed to press down all around her as she drove home. The storm was like the trouble with Jesse's letters: it loomed over her, it threatened, yet it refused to break.

She had toyed with the idea of telling Susan that Jesse didn't hate her, but she couldn't bring herself to do it. It was risky to present herself as Jesse's ally, knowing that he made Susan shudder. As an uninvited guest at the lunch table, Rainey's position wasn't secure. If Susan got annoyed, there was nothing to stop her from turning

Rainey in to Mr. Bennett. Then Rainey would be stuck in detention and, worse, would be sent back to her lunch table.

She wondered when Blake would crack and spill everything to Susan. She had been bracing herself for it all week, but it hadn't happened. She was beginning to wonder if he was capable of telling Susan to give him some space. But Susan was obviously getting to him. Whenever Susan leaned attentively in his direction, he shot an anguished glance at Rainey. She had even overheard him asking Shauna how she got her lunch period changed.

Just then a car horn sounded behind her. She jumped guiltily, afraid she had violated some rule of the road without realizing it.

A blue Ford pulled up abreast of her on the right and the driver's arm waved wildly out the window.

Rainey decided the other car was signaling her that something had dropped off her car, and as soon as she could she pulled off the road to count her hubcaps.

The Ford pulled over, too, and Michael got out. "I thought you'd never pull over, Rainey. I was waving. I was hollering. You live in a dream world, you know that?"

"You nearly gave me a heart attack! I thought something had fallen off my car."

He glanced at the car. "It's probably only a matter of time. But that's not why I stopped you. I have to talk to somebody and Blake's not at home. His mom says he's gone out to the florist to pick up a corsage. Did you know people still did that kind of thing?"

"Look, it's about to pour down rain. Do you mind coming to the point?"

"Ah, the sympathetic ear of a woman. Now listen carefully, Rainey, this is important—Cynthia knows how old I am and it doesn't matter to her!" Michael let out a little whoop of delight. "It was on my hospital admission slip. You remember—they had to X-ray me and all. She really just likes me as a person. I mean, we've gotten really close and all and she can see past all this superficial junk about age. What a woman!"

"I'm really happy for you, Michael."

"I had to tell somebody. I can't tell my parents, right? They still have this idea Cynthia's in high school. And stupid Blake is out getting carnations when I need him."

"You can always talk to me." Rainey smiled suddenly. "Now, how would you like to do *me* a favor?"

"Sure, Rainey. Anytime."

"Go with me to the dance tonight."

"What?"

"Well, you aren't taking Cynthia, are you?"

"Good grief, no. She's not interested in high-school dances. She's deep, sensitive."

"And too old."

Michael looked hurt. "She's not too old, man. She's just right. She's perfect. She's at the peak of young womanhood."

"Too old for high-school dances, I meant, that's all."

"I'd love to do you a favor, Rainey, but I hate that kind of social junk. Besides, I'm still in a cast. See? I can't dance."

"That's all right. You don't have to dance. All I need is a sort of warm body."

"Well, gee, thanks. I'm deeply flattered."

"I'll pick you up at seven-thirty," she said.

"But—"

"Don't worry, I won't bring you a corsage."

Rainey drove off before he could marshal any more objections. She was beginning to feel more cheerful already. She had noticed that she always perked up once she took some kind of action. When Michael reminded her of the dance, it hit her suddenly that if things were likely to blow up with Susan, Blake, and Jesse, it would happen that night. At dances there was no assigned seating, no regimentation. In a setting fraught with tension and the unreasonably high expectations a dance promoted, anything could happen. She wanted to be on the spot when it did, not sitting at home twiddling her thumbs and wondering what was going on.

As soon as Rainey got home, she leafed through her closet until she came upon the black crepe skirt she had had to buy for the Christmas concert a couple of years before. Paired with her best silky blouse, it would look okay for a dance. It only needed the right accessories. She took a can of spray paint out by the clothesline and sprayed her old beige sandals gold. The paint job wasn't quite perfect, but luckily the lights were always dim at dances. She already had a gold belt. With some rhinestone earrings and an artificial rose twisted in her hair she'd be fine. She felt a raindrop on her nose and scurried inside, bending over to protect the newly painted shoes from stray drops.

A cool wind was blowing when Jesse drove home. Dry leaves scudded across the clay road ahead of him, and his car was buffeted by the force of the wind as he pulled into his front yard. When he got out, the wind in the tall trees that edged the pasture behind the house sounded ominous. He had to squint to keep grit from blowing in his eyes. Glancing across the street, he saw Rainey dash out of her trailer, caught for a second in the light spilling from the open front door. Why was she dressed up, he wondered. The wind whipped her dark hair over her face and turned her umbrella inside out. She struggled to close it as she hurried to her car.

The cold raindrops blew against Jesse's face like a slap just then. The dance. The stupid fall dance. He had forgotten about it. Susan was going with Blake. Only the day before, he had overheard a couple of girls talking about what a glamorous couple they were.

He watched Rainey's old car drive down the road. Its headlights beamed against the woodlands beside the road, then it turned and vanished into darkness. He could hear the rain coming from the west.

When he turned to go inside, the lights of the farmhouse flickered. He paused a second, watching the raindrops hit the brightly lit windowpanes, then he went in.

His mother was in the kitchen. "I hope the electricity isn't going out," she said. "I wanted to do some sewing tonight." She was standing on a chair reaching for the candles that were kept on a high shelf. Jesse's father had gone hunting in the next county and would be gone all weekend. "Want something to eat, Jesse? There's fried chicken on the stove. And some potato salad in the icebox."

"Not now, Mom. I'm going out."

"Going out? How can you be going out? You just this second got back."

"Yeah, but now I'm going to a dance. It's kind of a last-minute thing. Is there plenty of hot water?"

"I guess. I was going to wait until after you ate before I turned on the dishwasher."

When Jesse got in the bathroom, he turned the shower on full force, filling the bathroom with steam. If he had had his way, they would have had one of those gigantic water heaters that let you take two- and three-hour showers. Not that he had the time for a long shower that night. He had to hurry. The dance had already started.

After he was bathed and dressed, his fair hair slicked back, the rain was still drumming steadily on the farmhouse roof.

His mother looked fretfully out the window. "It's really coming down now. I don't see why you have to go out on a night like this."

"Oh, come on, Mom, I'm not going to melt." He was determined to go to the dance because he had been struck by an encouraging idea. The city's electrical utilities were known to be unreliable in rainstorms. They were due to be modernized as soon as the city could float a bond. And if the lights went out, the dance would offer some interesting possibilities. He grabbed his car keys and headed out the front door. Smiling, he jumped in the Camaro and drove west, directly into the storm.

Meanwhile, Rainey had been squinting at street signs in Michael's neighborhood. The rain drove white against the car windows, making it almost impossible to see. She was forced to slow the car to a crawl. When at last she reached Michael's house, she pulled up in front and blew her horn. She puffed on her hands a little to warm them, anxiously wondering whether he would come out. After all, she had sort of pressured him to go with her.

Finally she saw a figure coming toward the car dimly lit by her headlights. Michael was wearing an old gray raincoat made for somebody far shorter. He threw open the car door and a gust of rain and wind blew in on her. "Lucky thing I've got a fiberglass cast," he said, falling awkwardly into the seat. "I'm already soaked."

A twinge of conscience hit Rainey when she saw Michael's cast, but she reminded herself that he had plenty of strength for chasing Cynthia and that it wouldn't kill him to go to a dance. The car windows were completely fogged over now and water dripped in pools on the floor and leaked into the torn upholstery, making it smell vaguely of dogs.

"Do you really think anybody's going to show up for this dance?" Michael asked her. "Wouldn't you rather get a hamburger or something instead?"

Rainey started the car. "People will show up. Everybody's going to be there. A dance is something people plan ahead for. They buy clothes and stuff. They aren't going to let a little rain stop them."

"I figured you'd say something like that. Well, I just hope this doesn't bring on a recurrence of my jungle fever."

"You have seen too many movies."

"An impossibility. Look, do you know how Steven Spielberg started out? Peter Bogdanovich? Watching old movies, that's how."

Rainey wiped the fog off the windshield with the back of her hand and peered anxiously at the road ahead. She didn't like the way she could hear water hitting the underside of the car as she plowed through puddles. Unconsciously, she began to edge the car toward the center of the road to avoid the puddles.

"T'ain't a fit night out for man, nor beast," Michael said. "W. C. Fields said that."

"I wish W. C. Fields were doing the driving tonight."

After a while she was able to edge her way out onto the thoroughfare. The wide avenue was a blur of bright lights, rain, and traffic. She could hear water spurting from under the wheels of cars as they passed her.

After driving some blocks along Sunset, she turned off onto Baker Street, the long road that led to the school. It was like plunging suddenly into darkness. The arc lights set far apart and the car's weak headlights were no match for the rain. Rainey couldn't even be sure where the edges of the road lay. She wiped her hand over the foggy windshield once more and clung to the steering wheel. She tried to concentrate on the broken white line running down the center, since that at least was relatively visible.

Michael wiped a patch clear on his window. "I think the ditches are overflowing. It must have started raining over here first. It's washing up on the road now."

"How far do you think we are from school?"

"Two, maybe three miles."

Rainey swore under her breath. She wiped her clammy hand with no result against her crepe skirt and gripped the steering wheel more tightly. "I wish we'd get there. The traction on these tires isn't the greatest. I think they're retreads."

Suddenly the lights of an oncoming car appeared ahead of them.

"Jeez, Rainey, I don't think he sees us. Pull over."

In a split second Rainey realized that the other driver must have been pulling toward the middle to avoid the overflowing ditches, just as she had. She braked and suddenly her car was hydroplaning. She could feel it sliding.

"Pump the brakes," Michael yelled.

They heard the sickening, crunching sound of one car hitting another and Rainey squeezed her eyes closed.

When she opened them, the rain was washing around them, drumming on the roof, driving into the windshield. Their car headlights shone crazily on shiny grass and a long broad wash of water.

"We hit them," Michael said.

"But where are they?"

"Probably we just grazed them." Michael twisted around in his seat belt. "Look, there they are. See their lights? They must have gone in the ditch on the other side."

Rainey was surprised that her car was still running. She put it in reverse and cautiously backed up. The rear wheels had never left the paved road, so she had no trouble righting it. She breathed a sigh of relief that she had not gone in the ditch. She hated to think what it would cost to have a wrecker pull her out. Then she inched the car cautiously forward.

"What are you doing?" yelped Michael.

"Counting my blessings," Rainey said grimly.

"Look, you can't leave the scene of an accident. Don't you remember all that stuff in the driver's booklet about that?"

"But, Michael, doesn't this kind of thing do something awful to your insurance rates?"

"This is no time to be thinking of something like that. The people in that other car could be hurt. They could be bleeding to death."

Rainey privately thought that if they were bleeding to death she didn't want to be there to see it, but she pushed that unworthy notion away. "Don't you think they're probably okay? It was just a glancing blow."

"You don't see them getting out of the car, do you?"

Rainey looked over her shoulder. "Well, it *is* pouring

rain. Besides, how do we know they haven't gotten out already?''

''We've got to check on them,'' Michael said firmly. ''They could be concussed.''

''Oh, all right.'' She stopped, leaving her lights on, and reached for her umbrella in the back seat.

''Do you have a flashlight in here anywhere?'' Michael asked.

''Try the glove compartment.''

Rainey slipped off her gold-painted shoes. She only wished she could peel off her panty hose as well. She made a face and opened her car door. ''I'll bet they're all going to be fine.''

It was pouring by the time Jesse got to the gym, but it had never occurred to him to wear a raincoat. He didn't even own one. He wore a leather jacket for protection against the elements, but his head always faced the weather bare. He got out of the car, pushed his wet hair out of his eyes, and made a dash for the entrance.

A withered-looking man stood at the door holding a sheaf of paper. ''Student I.D.?'' he said.

While Jesse reached for his wallet, his clothes dripped little puddles on the floor. The man checked his name off a computer list. ''And once you've left the dance,'' the man said flatly, ''you can't get back in the building.'' This precaution was obviously designed to keep students from getting drunk in the parking lot and then returning to the dance. Jesse paid little attention.

A flash of lightning cracked, the lights in the gym flickered, and a few girls squealed. Jesse looked up at the lights. The storm was on his side—he and the storm were one. He could hear the thunder in his heart. Something was going to happen tonight, something important. He was sure of it.

Susan had not seen Jesse come in. She shifted her weight uncomfortably, her legs feeling sticky inside her panty hose. She hated wet weather. It frizzed her hair, turning it dull and spongelike.

"Great decorations," said Blake.

"Thank you. We put a lot of effort into them."

Her glance skated lightly over Blake. There must be girls in the gym who were envying her. That idea, which had cheered her up at other low times in her life, wasn't helping now. She and Blake were standing in front of a trellis covered with autumn leaves, the greatest triumph of the decoration committee. Not entirely incidentally, it complimented Susan's coloring and she had made it a point to drift back and stand in front of it whenever possible. But now she wondered if it was worth the effort. Right then nothing seemed worth the effort.

"I hope the lights don't go out," said Blake.

"I hope not, too," said Susan. "That would be awful, with all these people in here."

"Maybe you'd like some punch," Blake suggested.

"That would be nice."

She had half a mind to ask Blake outright about the letters. But what was the point? It couldn't be more obvious that he hadn't written them. Ann Lee had been right about that. The kind of boy who wrote those letters was not the kind who stood around awkwardly talking about decorations. She was surprised she had not seen this obvious truth before.

Susan noticed that Blake actually looked more relaxed when he was walking away from her. She watched him joking with Jack Tyson, laughing. Why did he ask her to the dance, she thought resentfully, if he didn't want to stay with her?

The lights flickered, causing a little nervous laughter around the gym. A few feet behind the trellis, Jesse tensed and glanced upward. Why wouldn't they go out?

"I think it's letting up some," someone said. Thunder rumbled in the distance.

Blake returned with punch and cookies. When Susan bit into one of the large cookies, it suddenly disintegrated. Jesse watched as Blake brushed crumbs off her dress. Dark blood seemed to rise in his throat and Jesse's eyeballs felt swollen. He ached to put his hands around Blake's throat and give him a good shake. The worst part was Susan didn't even seem happy. He recognized the dejected slump of her shoulders. He looked away then, took a deep breath, and tried to think more calmly.

What he needed to do was to find somebody to dance with. He glanced around the gym swiftly, trying to find Rainey. She had come alone, he knew, and had left before he had. But the funny thing was there was no sign of her. He couldn't just stand there. He might start to look conspicuous, and he needed to stay close to Susan or the lights going out wouldn't do him any good. They usually weren't out for long.

"Hi, Jesse."

He wheeled around. "Oh, hi, Terri."

"D'you come by yourself?"

"Yeah."

"I came with Marty Hobson. He's gone to the bathroom." She laughed a little. "Want to dance?"

"Sure. Okay." In one way, it was too bad they were playing a slow dance, because he didn't want Terri to get any ideas. But in another way, it was a good thing because it made it easier for him to keep an eye on Susan and Blake. Terri took his hand and they began to move in time to the music. When she rested her cheek against his shoulder, he was scarcely conscious of it—Susan and Blake had started to dance, too.

"Ouch," said Terri. "That was my toe."

"Sorry."

She smiled up at him. "It's okay. I don't mind being stepped on by you, Jesse. We're old friends, right?"

He began to wonder if Terri had been slipped a swift belt of something stronger than punch.

He subtly guided her over to where he could see Blake's dark head amid a crowd of other couples, but that was as close as he could get without being obvious. He was relieved to see Marty Hobson coming back from the men's room.

"Hi, Jesse. Taking good care of my girl?"

"She's all yours, Marty." Jesse let go of Terri and moved away. He couldn't believe the way Terri looked at him as he walked away. Didn't she have any self-respect? What they had had was ancient history. How could she keep throwing herself at him?

Making his way off the dance floor, Jesse passed by Susan and Blake and felt himself go hot and cold all at once. Talk about self-respect. He guessed he was in no position to preach about it, was he? He sucked in a deep breath and looked up at the lights, but they kept beaming on in spite of all the thought waves he was sending them.

Two miles away, on Baker Street, Rainey and Michael were sloshing through the rain toward a disabled car. The pebbled road bit into Rainey's stockinged feet and muddy water squished uncomfortably between her toes. "I guess you realize this means we won't make it to the dance,'' she said gloomily.

"What is a dance when a fellow mortal's life may be at stake?"

"Right," said Rainey. "Of course, you're right." She had never been in an automobile accident before, but the pictures on the evening news had convinced her it was an experience she could do without. She just hoped there wouldn't be a lot of blood. The disabled car was resting with one wheel in the ditch. Its axle must be flat against the ground.

"Somebody's in there, all right," Michael said when they reached the car. "See? The windows are fogged. I wonder if the door's jammed." He pulled on the door handle and to Rainey's surprise the door came open at once. The light inside the car came on when the door opened, but with her standing behind Michael and the rain coming down, she couldn't see very well. Not that she tried very hard. She was still worried about there being a lot of blood.

"Are you okay?" Michael yelled. "Do we need to call an ambulance?"

"I am fine," said a raspy voice in icy tones. "I am only pausing a moment to collect myself. Do not trouble yourself."

"It's Mr. Bennett, Rainey!" Michael flashed a smile over his shoulder at Rainey. "I'm sure you're aware, sir, that all accidents have to be reported to the police. An accident report has to be filed and all. I know you've seen those accident reports in the papers."

"I do not need you to lecture me, Dessaseaux. Get out of my way."

Michael's substantial body blocked any closing of the

door. "Is that Mrs. Bennett over there, sir, cowering against the other door. Why, no! It's Bambi Whitney. How about that! You know Bambi, don't you, Rainey? I think it's just wonderful when a principal takes time away from school to consult with students."

A low growl in Mr. Bennett's throat made Rainey step away. She felt the headlights of an approaching car on her, and a station wagon pulled up beside her.

"Do you need help? Is anybody hurt?" called the driver.

"Would you look at that!" said Michael. "A stranger stopping to help. And they talk about the alienation of modern times!"

Rainey became conscious that the rain was slacking off. She could hear everything everyone was saying, for example, and her umbrella seemed to be working, at last. Rain was no longer whipping against her stockinged legs. She went over to the station wagon. "Would you call the police for us and report that there's been an accident?"

Michael was leaning against the open door of Mr. Bennett's disabled Ford. He seemed completely unconcerned about the rain, which was streaming down his face and soaking in around the edges of his inadequate raincoat. "And don't you worry, sir." He shifted his weight to his good foot. "Rainey and I will stay right here until the police come and the proper reports are filed with the authorities." He grinned happily at Rainey.

The storm was passing and still the lights had not gone out at the dance. With a feeling close to panic, Jesse saw his chance passing by. His hands grew cold and a pulse fluttered in his throat. This couldn't be happening. He backed away from the lights and the dancing couples and steadied himself against the wall, trying to think. Susan was standing alone again. He could see her over by that green wood thing. But what good did that do him if the lights wouldn't go out?

He gritted his teeth. The lights *had* to go out. If he had been able to go outside, he probably could have flung a hatchet or Bowie knife at the electric wires where they entered the building. He knew he could have hit the wires, and that would probably have knocked the lights out. But with that jerk of a cop standing by the door, he couldn't go outside and expect to get in again. Anyway, even if he could, even if he counted on the confusion of the darkness to cover his getting in, he couldn't very well cut the electric wires and leave them dangling over parked cars. That would be too dangerous.

He tensed suddenly. There had to be a simpler way to cut the electrical supply than by bringing down the wires.

He was near a short passageway where a mop and bucket stood forgotten. He was in a desolate, hidden corner of the gym that reflected his mood well enough, but now he perceived that it might offer an answer to his difficulties as well. He went over to the mop and bucket, looked around, and then pushed open a door next to it. A smell of mildew and disinfectant hit him. Buckets with wheels sat in the closet. On the shelves were green and yellow plastic containers of cleaning and waxing solutions. He shut the door behind him and switched on the bare bulb that illuminated the small room. It only took him a moment to find what he was looking for—the fuse box. He pulled it open and contemplated a row of circuit breakers. Without knowing what circuit went with what, he would have to flick them all off. He took a pen light out of his pocket and began flicking the circuits.

Suddenly the music stopped. A few girls screamed. "The lights are gone," someone yelled.

Jesse made his way out of the janitor's room, guided by the tiny pencil of light he held in his hand, and aimed for the trellis where Susan had been standing. He just hoped she hadn't moved.

A moment later he heard Susan's tremulous voice near him in the darkness. "I'm afraid to move. I might crash into the trellis. Blake?"

"Hang on, Susan," said Blake. "I'm going to try to get out to the car. There's something funny about this. Didn't you notice that they didn't all short out at once? This doesn't look like your normal electrical outage to me. I'm going to try to shine my headlights on the open door."

All around the gym, people were tripping over one another and bumping into one another, screaming. Jesse heard a sloshing sound and then a crash. He smiled. The punch bowl. He had a feeling it was going to take Blake longer than he thought to make it all the way across the gym and out to his car. He switched off his pen light and pocketed it.

"Don't move, anybody!" shrieked Ann Lee. "There might be broken glass. You might slip on the wet floor. Stay still! I'm going to try to find a flashlight!"

"I think I'll just stay right here," Susan said in a small voice.

Jesse drew close to her. He could feel the warmth of her bare arms next to him. "Susan," he said huskily.

"Blake?" she said uncertainly.

"No, not Blake." He put his hands on her arms, drew her close to him, and kissed her. His blood was pounding in his ears with excitement.

"Whaa?" said Susan's muffled voice.

"Don't talk, okay?" He put his arms around her and held her tight. He was overwhelmed by the closeness of her, the apple smell of her hair, her warm softness. "I love you, I never want to let you go. I hope the stupid lights stay out all night," he murmured.

"J-Jesse? *You* wrote those letters?"

He kissed her again. It was the most satisfying moment he had had for six months, even including the shutout in the East Gate–West Mount game. It was like two people melting together, with no feuds separating them. "I love your hair," he murmured, running his fingers through it. "I love the smell of you."

"People!" a voice shrieked almost in his ear. "I've got a flashlight!"

A bright beam of light shone blindingly in their eyes.

"Jesse?" said Ann Lee. "Susan?"

Jesse swore softly. With a quick intake of his breath he fled. He could hear a motor starting outside. It was only a question of time until headlights flared in the open double doors. Catlike, he made his way through the confused mob in the gym. Somebody near him giggled.

"I can't believe this," he heard somebody say. "I mean, this is what it's like to live under West Mount Electric Company. There ought to be an investigation or something. Our dance—ouch!"

"Go along the walls," a deep voice said. "That way you at least know where you're going—*ooph!*"

"For crying out loud, would you take it easy?"

Jesse left the confused voices behind him. Outside, the air was cool and rinsed clean. The rain had stopped. He smiled up at the crescent moon, which had surfaced from behind a cloud. *If I die tomorrow*, he thought, *if every-*

body finds out and I get thrown out of school for good, it was worth it.

He got in his car, slammed the door closed, and drove out of the lot. He was driving off just as Rainey, in her ancient car, pulled in, but he scarcely noticed. He felt loose. He felt great. He was on a roll. He was a winner. It was only as his car turned onto the well-lit thoroughfare of Sunset Avenue that a quiet and troubling thought hit him. Susan hadn't pushed him away and she hadn't seemed to hate him. That was good. But *what was going to happen next?* Had anything really changed?

Rainey drove into the packed parking lot. "What's going on?" she said. "The lights are out. Look, Michael, the whole gym is dark!"

"Another one of these dumb electrical outages."

But Rainey noticed that the neighborhood past the school was lit. The streetlights were on and all the exterior school lights were on. Lights were on everywhere but in the gym. "Something's going on," she said.

Rainey saw that Blake's Corvette was parked so that its headlights shone square on the open double doors of the gym. It was obvious that the dance was breaking up. Chaperones were standing at the entrance, blinking in the light. A few kids were already walking to their cars.

"What happened?" Michael yelled out the window.

"Dance is over." A boy shrugged. "Electricity went out."

"We missed it!" Rainey cried. "Something finally happened and we missed it."

Michael got out of the car. "Blake! Blake, old buddy! What's going on?"

Rainey got out and trailed after him.

"I don't know," Blake said. "It was funny. The lights went out one by one. It was really strange. Hey, Susan, let me get that door." A dazed-looking Susan scrambled into the Corvette.

Rainey bent down to talk to her through the car window. "What happened, Susan? You were there the whole time, weren't you?"

Susan's eyes were blank. "Well—the punch bowl broke."

"Went down with a crash," Blake affirmed. "Ann Lee is falling to pieces in there."

"Well, she did get pretty wet, Blake." Susan smoothed her polka-dotted skirt.

"People are bumping into one another all over the place. It's a circus," said Blake. "Poor Susan was scared out of her mind."

"Not really," she demurred.

He didn't seem to hear her. "I knew something funny was happening right away. I said, 'Something tells me this is no ordinary blackout,' didn't I, Susan?"

"Sabotage?" suggested Michael. "Is that what you're telling me?"

Ann Lee came up to them. The skirt of her blue dress was drenched in front and her hair looked wild. "Why would anybody want to sabotage the only dance we've had all year?" she cried. "The dance we worked on and slaved over. I can't believe it's sabotage."

Susan was carefully pleating her skirt with her fingers. "Certainly not," she said. "What motive would anybody have?" She and Ann Lee exchanged a long look in silence.

Rainey knew something was going on, but for once she couldn't quite figure out what.

FIFTEEN

At school on Monday Michael slapped Rainey on the shoulder. Getting slapped by Michael was a sensation rather like getting bumped by a truck. "Cut it out," she protested feebly.

"Didn't I tell you you'd never be sorry you stopped to help those poor unfortunates we hit?"

"We didn't hit them, Michael. They hit us."

"Same difference."

"Not to the police and the insurance company."

"We're heroes! What'd I tell you? Jeremy Burns—his dad's on the school board—called me last night and told me Mr. Bennett plans to apply for a leave of absence. How about that?"

"It's good, all right."

"No more assigned seating, no more vigilante patrolling of the parking lot and the lunchroom. And it's all thanks to us."

"You really think?"

"Come on, when I explained it all, my dad said Mr. Bennett really didn't have any choice. Once the accident report turns up in the paper, the board was going to have to ask for his resignation anyway. They can't condone fraternization with the students. Man, that's just not done. I mean, it stands to reason. Can you imagine a high school where the principal dates the students? The thing you've got to understand, Rainey, is that we have these rules for a reason. My dad spoke on this theme for an hour, an hour and a half maybe. He was really shocked."

"Your parents don't know about Cynthia yet, huh?"

"I'm working up to it." Michael grinned. "But with Cynthia and me, the difference in our age is tiny—purely technical. It's just not at all the same thing, Rainey."

"Hey, Rainey—good going!" A bunch of kids converged on them. A boy in a letter sweater wrung Rainey's hand. "Congratulations," he said. "Man, this is the greatest." Rainey stared at him blankly. She had never seen him before in her life.

"If directing movies doesn't work out for me," Michael said thoughtfully, "I might try being a press agent."

A girl grabbed Rainey's arm and wheeled her around. It was Amy Snell from her chemistry class. "Is it true? Mr. Bennett is leaving?"

Rainey nodded.

Amy embraced her. "Do you realize what this means?"

"No more assigned lunchroom seating," someone chimed in.

"Freedom!" a voice from the back of the crowd shouted.

The bell sounded, and to Rainey's relief the crowd of kids around her began to break up.

Michael pounded her on the back again. "You've got to get used to it, Rainey. You're a hero. The way you rammed Bennett's car! The way you skewered the crumb, caught in his own hypocrisy—jeez, it was great." His eyes took on a spacey look. "Hey, I think this could be my creative-writing project. I've got my idea at last. An epic poem! Yes, I can see it! The Raineiad!"

Rainey backed away and made her escape. What was an epic poem, anyway? At least it didn't sound like anything that was actually embarrassing. Her mind was spinning so fast that she accidentally went past her homeroom and found herself at the end of A wing. The locker alcove was all but deserted. Only one couple lingered there. Rainey blinked rapidly as she recognized Susan and Jesse. Jesse's arm was outstretched against the locker and he was looking down into Susan's face with an expression so personal that Rainey, her face hot, pivoted sharply and retreated. Jesse and Susan? Those love letters had evidently worked.

Jesse and Susan did not hear Rainey's retreating footsteps.

"I love you, too," Susan said. "The letters, and—well, I guess I loved you all along, that's all."

Jesse kissed her lightly on the forehead.

"We're going to be late to class," Susan said. But she looked pleased.

"I don't care. Can't I kiss my girl as much as I want?"

Susan smiled. "Then I guess we're going to be late to class."

"Mmm. I guess so," said Jesse.

Mitzi Freemont overtook Rainey in the hall. "Did you see Jesse McCracken and Susan Brantley making out back there? I thought they hated each other."

"Not exactly," said Rainey.

"I heard that the dance was a total disaster and that somebody sabotaged the lights and that Mr. Bennett is turning in his resignation."

"You've got it about right."

"I can't believe my parents made me go with them to my grandmother's dumb eightieth birthday party this weekend. I miss out on everything."

"I know the feeling."

"How can you say that? Michael told me you went to the dance with him and that you rammed Mr. Bennett's car and now you say you missed out? You were right in the middle of it."

Rainey scarcely heard Mitzi. Watching Jesse and Susan in the locker alcove, she felt she had had a glimpse of a profound mystery—love. She wanted to try it out herself. To think that a few weeks ago all she had wanted was a car. Something told her that love was going to be a bit trickier than getting a car.

When Rainey stepped into her homeroom a spontaneous cheer broke out and she sat down abruptly, feeling confused.

"Hooray!" someone shouted.

"Class," said Mrs. Armstrong. "Calm down." But Rainey could see she was struggling to hide a smile.

While Mrs. Armstrong called the roll, Rainey wrote

in block letters on her notebook, ''LOVE.'' She stared at it.

''Rainey Locklear,'' said Mrs. Armstrong.

''Here,'' said Rainey absently. She retraced the block letters with her pen. Love? Why not? She would work on that next. After all, stranger things had already happened at West Mount High.

To find out what happens next at West Mount High, look for *Easy Answers*, coming in March 1990.

About the Author

JANICE HARRELL decided she wanted to be a writer when she was in the fourth grade. She grew up in Florida and received her master's and doctorate degrees in eighteenth-century English literature from the University of Florida. After teaching college English for a number of years, she began to write full time.

She lives in Rocky Mount, North Carolina, with her husband, a psychologist, and their daughter. Ms. Harrell is a compulsive traveler—some of the countries she has visited are Greece, France, Egypt, Italy, England, and Spain—and she loves taking photographs.